How she chose to live her life was none of his business!

There was no way Fiona intended to defend her lifestyle to Craig. Her jaw tightened angrily as she glared back at him. "I really don't think I'll need to make any changes in my living arrangements."

Craig's smile widened. "You don't? I admire your optimism."

"Do you? How nice." Fiona's tone was brittle. "I wish I could say that I saw something to admire in you. But I'm afraid I can't. Not one single thing."

"Not even when you employ those legendary sharp eyes of yours?"

"Not even when I employ my even more legendary imagination."

Stephanie Howard is a British author whose two ambitions since childhood were to see the world and to write. Her first venture became a four-year stay in Italy, learning the language and supporting herself by writing short stories. Then her sensible side brought her back to London to study Social Administrations at the London School of Economics. She has held various editorial posts at magazines such as *Reader's Digest*, *Vanity Fair*, and *Women's Own*. She has also written free-lance for *Cosmopolitan*, *Good Housekeeping* and *The Observer*.

Books by Stephanie Howard

HARLEQUIN ROMANCE
3112—AN IMPOSSIBLE PASSION
3153—WICKED DECEIVER
3195—ROMANTIC JOURNEY
3220—A MATTER OF HONOUR
3237—DANGEROUS INFATUATION
3247—A ROMAN MARRIAGE

HARLEQUIN PRESENTS
1098—RELUCTANT PRISONER
1130—DARK LUCIFER
1168—HIGHLAND TURMOIL
1273—BRIDE FOR A PRICE
1307—KISS OF THE FALCON
1450—A BRIDE FOR STRATHALLANE

Don't miss any of our special offers. Write to us at the following address for information on our newest releases.

Harlequin Reader Service
P.O. Box 1397, Buffalo, NY 14240
Canadian address: P.O. Box 603,
Fort Erie, Ont. L2A 5X3

UNCHAIN MY HEART
Stephanie Howard

Harlequin Books

TORONTO • NEW YORK • LONDON
AMSTERDAM • PARIS • SYDNEY • HAMBURG
STOCKHOLM • ATHENS • TOKYO • MILAN
MADRID • WARSAW • BUDAPEST • AUCKLAND

ISBN 0-373-17160-9

UNCHAIN MY HEART

CHAPTER ONE

FIONA was still inwardly quivering with anger when the internal phone on her desk began to ring.

She snatched it to her ear. 'Yes?' she demanded crisply. If it was Hamish, she would refuse point-blank to speak to him. And if he insisted, she would simply hang up on him.

It wasn't Hamish, it was Hamish's secretary.

'Mr Campbell would like a word with you, Miss MacGregor.' The girl began to elaborate. 'I mean Mr——'

But Fiona cut in impatiently. 'I'm sorry, Sheena, I'm terribly busy at the moment. Please tell Mr Campbell that he'll simply have to wait until our meeting this afternoon.'

She replaced the receiver with a firm, decisive click, yet she was aware that her hands were still trembling slightly. Damn Hamish Campbell! Damn his insolent persistence! What did it take to convince him that she was sick of his pestering?

In an effort to calm herself, she rose from her desk and crossed to the window, taking deep, slow breaths. These episodes with Hamish were starting to get to her, for the truth was she didn't quite know how to handle them.

Fiona smiled wryly. That really wasn't like her. Over the years she had learned how to handle most things.

5

A light frown touched her brow as she gazed out of the window at the stretching silent landscape of freshly fallen snow. It had been snowing for three days now, a few flakes were still falling, and the hills of Glen Almond off to the north were shrouded in a deep, thick mantle of purest white.

She sighed. It was so beautiful, even in mid-February, though winter was not her favourite time of year. And she paused for a moment to lean against the window-sill and push back the silky fall of hair from her face—hair almost as pale as the very snow itself, that framed her delicate honey-skinned features in a soft, immaculate bob to her shoulders and set off to perfection her wide violet eyes.

Her soft, full mouth pursed tightly for a moment. She loved this place, here in the heart of Perthshire, these hills, that stunning Scottish landscape; she loved them just as much as her dear father had done. And she loved, too, the furniture manufacturing business of which, on his recent death, he had bequeathed her his precious share. No one, and certainly not Hamish Campbell, whatever tactics he might choose to employ against her, would ever succeed in pushing her out!

'I thought you were supposed to be terribly busy? You don't look terribly busy to me.'

At the sound of a male voice coming from the doorway, Fiona swung round, her heart jumping inside her. She knew that voice. It sent a cold chill through her. So, she thought cynically, big brother's been sent for. Hamish has called in the heavy brigade!

'Hello, Craig.' She looked into his face, and with an effort kept her tone flat, unemotional. Yet there was the tiniest hint of acid as she added, 'What brings you to this unlikely neck of the woods?'

As she spoke, quite unconsciously, she quickly reached up and tucked a strand of hair behind one ear. It was a reflex action, a sign of nervous tension. She always did it when she felt anxious or afraid.

He was standing watching her from the doorway, hands pushed casually into the trouser pockets of the sharply cut dark navy suit he was wearing. It was three years since she had last set eyes on him, more like five since they had last spoken, yet, to judge by the feelings that surged up inside her, their last encounter could have been yesterday.

Nothing had changed, she decided with a shiver, as in quick succession two thoughts occurred to her. He was still as heartbreakingly handsome as ever— the head of wavy hair as black as midnight, the endless deep dark eyes that seemed to look right through you, the straight proud nose, the firm square jawline, and that way he had of holding himself, as arrogant as some ancient chieftain warrior of old.

That was the first thought, instantly overtaken by the second—that the hatred she had always felt for him still burned as fiercely as ever.

'You look different.' Craig was still standing in the doorway, his tall, powerful frame seeming to fill the space around him. And, as he watched her with those long-lashed, shrewd black eyes of his, that familiar expression of amused superiority played at the corners of his wide, well-shaped mouth. It was a look, Fiona remembered, that in the insecure days of her childhood had been capable of reducing her to a state of tortured misery.

He smiled, still watching her. 'You've changed. For the better.'

'Have I?' The violet eyes looked unblinkingly back at him. 'I wish I could say the same of you.'

Craig's smile simply widened, to Fiona's irritation. By the look of things, he really hadn't changed one bit. He was as totally immune to her insults as ever.

'You've filled out a little, and in all the right places.' He stepped inside her office as he said it, his gaze skimming over her slim, lithe figure with its full, high breasts and softly flaring hips, flatteringly moulded in the simple lines of the violet cashmere tube-dress she was wearing. 'And you suit your hair a little shorter. It gives you a chic, sophisticated look.'

'Don't patronise me, Craig.' The violet eyes narrowed. A snap of anger stiffened her tone of voice. 'I don't need your assessment of how I look.'

'Not even when that assessment is so unequivocally complimentary?' The black eyes were dancing as he said it. 'I thought all women thrived on compliments?'

'It depends on the source.' Fiona's eyes looked right through him. 'Coming from you, compliments somehow lose their sparkle.'

The trouble with Craig was that he was all too aware of the power he was capable of wielding over women. In spite of her condemnation, he knew as well as she did that a compliment from a man of

such lethal good looks was destined to set any poor
female heart racing.

Any but mine, Fiona thought with satisfaction.
The only emotion he's capable of stirring in my
heart is the same emotion that I stir in his. Hatred.
Pure and simple.

He came to a halt just a few feet from her desk
and glanced past her through the window at the
snow-clad landscape.

Without looking at her, he observed, 'When you
told my brother's secretary you were too busy to
see me, I didn't expect to find you gazing out of
the window.' He slid a quick, cutting glance in her
direction. 'Perhaps you were seeking inspiration?'

Fiona ignored that. 'I didn't know it was you.
When she said Mr Campbell I assumed it was
Hamish.'

'So I gather. If you had given the girl a chance,
instead of so rudely interrupting her, she was on
the point of telling you which Mr Campbell she was
referring to.'

Craig's tone had sharpened. He threw her a
narrow look. 'So why were you so quick to refuse
to see my brother? I get the impression you would
not have been too busy to see anyone else.'

He was absolutely right, but there was no reason
for him to know that. He would only demand to
know the reason why. And that was something she
had no intention of telling him. It would only make
her problems with Hamish worse.

Fiona took refuge in evasion, as she turned away
and seated herself behind her big mahogany desk.
'There was no reason for Hamish to see me right

now. We had a brief meeting just over half an hour ago and we have another one scheduled for after lunch.'

'So I understand.' Craig's dark eyes were un-blinking. Still watching her, he slid his hands from his trouser pockets, reached for one of the high-backed chairs that stood in a semi-circle round the front of her desk, and lifted it forward a couple of feet before lowering his tall frame unhurriedly on to it. 'I hope you don't mind, but I'll be joining you.'

'At the directors' meeting? Why should I mind? After all, you're chairman of the company. I'd say you have a perfect right to join us.'

'I'd say so, too.' He held her eyes. 'And perhaps it's time I started taking a more active part in the running of the company.'

'Is that why you're here?' Fiona felt her heart lurch, though she managed to keep her anxiety from showing. This was what she'd feared the moment she'd set eyes on him standing in the doorway of her office. He'd arrived on the scene to back up his brother in his fight to squeeze her out.

She quickly pushed a strand of hair behind her ear, her free hand beneath the desk clenching tightly. A fight against Hamish would be hard, but within her power. She disliked and despised him, but she sensed she could beat him. A fight against Craig would be another matter entirely. He was made of much grittier stuff than his brother.

He sat back in his seat now and answered her question. 'Yes, that's why I'm here. To keep a closer eye on operations for a while.' He smiled an oblique smile. 'It seems, from what I've been hearing, that my presence is rather badly needed.'

'I reckon it must be for you to tear yourself away from the high-powered life you lead down in London these days.'

Fiona glared across at him, masking her fear with mockery. What exactly had he meant by that 'from what I've been hearing'? The remark, and the casual way he'd said it, had had a decidedly sinister ring. But, for the moment, she decided, she would let it pass.

She kept her tone lightly dismissive as she added, 'How on earth will the Campbell empire manage to keep going without you?'

'It may not.' He returned her mockery with amusement. 'But that's a risk I'll just have to take.' He stretched his legs out casually in front of him. 'And it's not quite an empire. At least, not yet.'

His smile as he uttered those last few words, just for an instant, shot Fiona back into the past. Though she had always hated him, she had also always admired his ambition and his unwavering conviction that he would succeed. It was a sign of his arrogance, but it was what drove him forward, and it was the single aspect of his character that she had sought, as she grew up, to adopt as her own.

To believe in oneself. That was what mattered.

But as she looked back at him now there was no hint of admiration. On the contrary, her tone was scathing as she put to him, 'Don't you think you're in danger of becoming a little greedy? To most people a chain of five-star hotels, an airline and a string of top-class restaurants...not to mention, of course, your share in this company...would more than classify as an adequate empire.'

'Ah, but I'm not most people. I thought you knew that.' The dark eyes danced, amused and arrogant, openly revelling in the disapproval they met. 'My definition of adequate is a little different from most people's.'

'So, is that why you're here?' She changed the subject abruptly. She sensed it pleased him too much to talk of his successes. 'Do you find the way Hamish runs this small fragment of your empire for you less than adequate, not to your liking? Have you come up to Inverairnie to pull him into line?'

Fiona smiled sarcastically as she said it, deliberately underlining the dig. They both knew that, whatever else he might have to tell her, she would hear no criticism of Hamish from him. Hamish, all his life, had been Craig's obedient little mouthpiece and Craig, in turn, his faithful defender. It was why Hamish had always got away with murder. For to challenge Hamish was to challenge his older brother, and very few people had the nerve to do that.

Nothing had changed to judge from Craig's response now. The smile had gone. He put to her coolly, 'Is there any reason why I should be displeased with my brother's performance as managing director of this company?' One straight black eyebrow lifted in challenge. 'If there is, I would very much like to hear it. I'm certainly not aware of any reason myself.'

Fiona had to concede, reluctantly, that neither was she. She shrugged. 'He does a reasonable job on the whole. Although there are certain areas in which we are not in agreement.'

'So I understand.' The dark eyes bored into her. 'But my brother has a little more experience than you do in the running of Birnam Wood Quality Repro. He's been working here for seven years compared to your three.'

'Four,' Fiona corrected him. 'I've been working here for four years. And I really think that's long enough to have earned a say in the running of the company.'

'Surely, as a shareholder, you have your say?'

'Certainly, I have my say.' She paused and pierced him with a look. 'But, invariably, my say is overruled. My forty per cent share in Birnam Wood Repro doesn't carry much clout when it's consistently up against Hamish's ten per cent combined with your fifty. And Hamish knows he has your backing in whatever he does. He knows he doesn't have to listen to me.'

Craig regarded her in silence for a moment, his strong arms folded across his broad chest. And why was it, Fiona wondered with a flash of irritation, that, in spite of the fact that, ensconced behind her desk, she was the one, supposedly, in a position of power, he still managed to look as though it was he who was in charge? It was that aura he carried with him of implacable authority, that ability to dominate, merely by his presence, whatever situation he was in.

Fiona straightened in her seat and sought to look down on him as he answered at last, his tone faintly damning, 'How come we're suddenly faced with all these disagreements? I can remember no such aggravation when your father was alive. He and Hamish seemed to get along without any trouble.'

At his words Fiona felt herself shrink a little inwardly. The loss of her father was still raw and painful. After all, it had barely been a year.

She pulled herself together. 'As I recall, Hamish did not oppose as a matter of course every suggestion my father put forward. My father's opinions were treated with respect, just as they were in the old days before your own father died.'

'And your opinions are not. Is that what you're implying?'

'I'm not *implying* anything. I'm being perfectly straight about it. Nobody's opinions except Hamish's are even considered. This company is no longer run the way it used to be.'

How could it be? she mused privately with a frown. Old Fergus Campbell and her father had been friends. She and the Campbell heirs would never be that.

Craig was watching her, unmoved. 'Alas, things change.'

'Must they change for the worse?' Her eyes flickered with resentment. 'Do you really think it's right that one of the company's directors can't even get a decent hearing for her ideas?'

Unhurriedly, still watching her, Craig unfolded his arms and laid them along the arms of his chair, his long tanned fingers cupping the curved ends.

'Perhaps,' he put to her, his tone as cold as ice-water, 'these ideas of yours that you're making such a fuss about do not merit being granted a decent hearing.'

'Who says they don't?' Fiona snapped the question at him. 'Who's been telling you these lies? Is it your brother?'

'I am unaware that my brother has been telling me lies.' Craig's tone was low, laced with cool warning. She might have known he would leap at once to defend Hamish!

She straightened her shoulders. 'Well, he has, I can assure you, if he's been suggesting that my input into this firm is not worth taking seriously. In the two years since I've been in charge of sales and marketing, our sales figures have risen by fifty per cent.'

Let him check the figures, if he didn't believe her! The proof was in the ledgers in irrefutable black and white!

'I'm aware of that.' He looked back at her steadily. 'But may I suggest that one of the reasons for that success is that my brother has managed to restrain you from implementing the series of dangerously madcap ideas that you have insisted on putting forward over the years?'

'Madcap ideas?' Surely she was hearing things? 'What sort of madcap ideas are you talking about?'

'I understand that there have been several.'

'Name one!' she demanded.

Craig smiled infuriatingly. 'Do I take it from this display of outrage that you deny the allegation?'

'Of course I deny it!'

'Yes, that was rather to be expected.'

'I deny it because there's not a shred of truth in it!' His calm tone, his smug smile were downright infuriating. Fiona leaned across the desk towards him and narrowed her eyes angrily. 'Name one instance to support your allegation! Go on! Just one!' she challenged fiercely. Then she sat back and waited. She knew he could not do it.

Her confidence, however, proved to be optimistic.

Craig seemed to settle himself more comfortably in his chair, crossing his long legs at the ankles. He took a deep breath. 'Try this one for size. I believe you put forward an inspired proposal to rename the various ranges of furniture we produce...? Didn't you suggest we drop their current names, the names they have been known by to the public for decades, and rename them all after flowers instead?'

Fiona blinked at him, disbelieving. 'Surely you're not serious? That was a joke. Hamish knew it was a joke. It sprang out of something my housekeeper said. My housekeeper, Iris...' She stopped midstream. Why should she feel obliged to explain something so silly? She sat back in her chair and took a deep breath. 'It was never intended as a serious proposition.'

'Hamish says it was.'

'Then Hamish is lying. Or else he's an idiot.' She looked Craig straight in the eye as she said it. It was time someone spoke the truth about his brother.

There was a momentary flicker at the back of the dark eyes, a flicker of warning, a silent staking of boundaries. Then Craig raised dark eyebrows and looked across at her levelly. 'And why should my brother lie to me?' he queried.

'To blacken my name. To put you against me.' The words came out calmly, more calmly than she felt. 'Surely you must know that Hamish wants rid of me? He wants me out of the company altogether.'

'If he does—and he has expressed no such desire to me—the only reason he could possibly have is the belief that you're simply not up to the job.'

'Is that what he's told you?' Fiona's stomach clenched. Suddenly, she felt seriously threatened. 'Well, that's a lie as well. I happen to be very good at my job...and I object very strongly to the slander that I'm not.'

She pushed a tendril of ash-blonde hair behind her ear, quite unaware that she was doing it. 'If you want to know the real reason behind Hamish's lies about me, I'll tell you, and it has nothing to do with the quality of my work...'

'And what has it to do with?' Craig smiled a scathing smile. 'Enlighten me. I'm interested,' he told her.

Fiona took a deep breath, struggling to calm her emotions. If she spoke calmly and rationally, perhaps he would listen.

'What it has to do with is power,' she told him quietly. 'Hamish isn't like you; he doesn't want an empire. He knows he isn't capable of anything like that. But he wants control of Birnam Wood Repro. He wants the freedom to run it his way.'

There was a pause. 'According to you, he already does that.'

'In effect, he does, thanks to the fact that he has your automatic backing. But I'm a bother to him. I refuse to let him walk all over me—even though, in the end, he usually gets his way. He hates the fact that I have any say at all. He wants rid of me. That's why he's told you these lies. He wants me out. I'm a thorn in his side.'

Momentarily, she was tempted to blurt out the rest, to tell him about the new form of harassment that Hamish had recently adopted against her. She was glad that she hadn't when, with a dismissive smile, Craig answered, 'I see you're a believer in that fine old adage that attack is the best form of defence. But answer me this. Has it never occurred to you that the only reason for my brother's opposition to you is that, as a family man, he has to think of the future, that he simply has the good of the company at heart?'

Her answer to that was simple. 'No, as a matter of fact it hasn't. If he had the good of the company at heart, he wouldn't be trying to stir up trouble within it.'

She looked into Craig's face, her gaze unwavering, yet aware of a leaden weight in her heart. To describe what was happening merely as 'trouble' was a somewhat casual understatement. Her future was at stake here, and, with Craig now ranked against her, what hope of surviving did she have?

Impatiently, she glanced away, remembering on a wave of anger the cruelty of which she knew he was capable, the cruelty that, as a child, had almost destroyed her. And, as always, that most memorable cruelty of all, the taunt that her parents were not her real parents, that she was adopted, that she did not really belong, sprang with claws bared into her mind.

Even now, those childhood memories could wound her, though she had long ago cast off the sense of insecurity that, as a vulnerable child, those taunts had stirred in her heart.

She looked at Craig now, eyes dark with resentment. His brother, Hamish, was nasty and despicable, but it was Craig she had always hated and feared. Craig was dangerous. He was the kind of man who was capable of sticking the knife in without the smile ever leaving his face.

He was smiling at her now. 'Perhaps I ought to warn you that pointing your finger at my brother and calling him a liar is not really going to get you very far.' He stood up slowly to face her squarely across the desk, pushing his hands into the pockets of his trousers.

'And there's one more point I really ought to warn you about... Like my brother, I have no time for incompetence. Those who aren't up to the job, whatever position they may hold, I promise you, will be ruthlessly weeded out.'

'Are you through with your warnings?' Fiona glared back at him hotly. How dared he threaten her like that?

He continued to smile at her, that cool, menacing smile of his. 'For the moment,' he answered. He nodded. 'For the moment.'

Then, as it seemed he was about to turn and leave, he paused for an instant to cast a quick glance out of the window. 'It's still snowing,' he observed, his tone conversational, as though concluding a perfectly amicable exchange. 'It looks as though it's going to be good skiing weather.'

To her annoyance, Fiona found herself, quite involuntarily, swivelling round to follow his gaze. By the time she had snapped back again he had gone from the room and the door was closing with a sharp click behind him.

CHAPTER TWO

FOR a long time after Craig had left the room Fiona remained seated at her desk, staring unseeingly at the blotter, her fingers unconsciously fiddling with the paper-knife.

She might have known Craig would arrive to back up his brother, to fight the battle Hamish was not capable of winning on his own. Hadn't it always been that way, ever since they were children?

A memory came to her of an incident long ago when a crowd of children, herself included, had been playing one summer's day in the Campbells' garden. Hamish had picked a fight with a little boy with glasses who had proved a tougher adversary than he'd bargained for. In tears, he'd gone screaming off to find Craig and five minutes later had returned with him in tow.

'Leave my brother alone.' That was all Craig had said to the boy in glasses, but it had been enough to put the fear of God in him. After that, Hamish had got his way for the rest of the afternoon.

And now, she sighed, though they were no longer children, it looked as though nothing had changed.

Nothing. She shivered. Not only was he still his brother's defender, but he was still more than capable of inflicting deadly wounds.

Her fingers froze around the handle of the paper-knife, as with a force that was still capable of ren-

dering her breathless the memory flooded back to
her, as fresh as though it were yesterday, of that
most deadly wound of all.

She'd been seven years old when Hamish had
tossed the bombshell at her. For in those days Craig
had used Hamish as his mouthpiece, his go-between
when he wished to perpetrate evil.

She and Hamish had been playing in the
Campbells' back garden, an innocent game of
skittles, she remembered. She had been winning—
in fact, she'd won three games in a row—when suddenly Hamish turned to her and smiled at her pity-
ingly. 'You realise you're only winning because I
let you win?'

Fiona hadn't believed him. 'And why would you
do that?'

He'd paused for only an instant. 'Because I feel
sorry for you. Craig says everybody ought to feel
sorry for you. After all,' he'd added artfully, 'it's
not your fault.'

'What's not my fault? And why should you feel
sorry for me?' Fiona had been genuinely baffled,
and at that stage quite unsuspecting of what was
to come.

'Because you're different.' He had regarded her
slyly. 'You're not like Craig and me. You're not
like other children.'

By that point Fiona's curiosity had been aroused,
and so too had a tiny prick of foreboding. 'Why
do you say that?' she had demanded, frowning.
'Why am I not like other children?'

To this day she could remember how he'd turned
away, then slid her a look that had sent shivers

through her. 'I can't tell you that,' he had answered, looking away again. 'Craig said I should, but maybe I shouldn't. Forget it. Please don't force me to tell you.'

'Tell me what?' In spite of her fear, she had insisted. She had tugged at his sleeve. 'Tell me, Hamish.'

He had turned once more to face her, feigning reluctance. 'Are you sure you really want to know?'

'I'm sure. Please tell me.'

'Don't tell anyone I told you.'

'I won't.' She had waited with bated breath.

And then he had said it, his green eyes innocent, as though unaware that he was crushing her heart. 'You're adopted. Your real parents died when you were born. The ones you have now aren't your real parents at all. They only took you in because they were sorry for you.'

As she had stood there, reeling, struggling to catch her breath, from an upstairs window Mrs Campbell had called for Hamish.

'My mother wants me. My *real* mother,' he'd emphasised, rubbing salt into her gaping, bleeding wound. And then he'd run off inside and left her.

Fiona had no idea how long she'd stood there. When, eventually, on legs almost too numb to carry her, she had made her way back to the house, she'd found Hamish and Craig sitting together playing a game of 'Snap' at the kitchen table.

As she'd walked into the room, her cheeks as pale as parchment, Hamish had glanced up at her, then turned to his thirteen-year-old brother, a look of belated remorse on his face. 'Perhaps I shouldn't have told her. She looks like a ghost. Perhaps we should have left it to her mother.'

'She'll get over it.' Craig was smirking hatefully. 'After all, she had to find out some time.'

Fiona remembered looking back at him, at that cruel, handsome face, unlike his younger brother's quite devoid of all remorse, and through the pain and the sickness churning inside her she had known with total certainty just how much he hated her.

And she had known, too, that, though it was Hamish who had struck the blow, it was Craig who had been the force behind it. Both brothers were evil, but Hamish was the weak one. Even at the age of seven, she had instinctively known that, and for that reason she had never seriously considered him a threat.

Craig was different. Craig was strong—both in character and in intellect. And evil combined with strength was a force to be reckoned with.

As the silver paper-knife slid from her fingers and rolled across the blotter to the edge of the desk, Fiona caught it quickly before it could drop off and snatched her thoughts abruptly back to the present.

The years had been peppered with cruel moments such as these, years during which her hatred for Craig Campbell had grown and flourished like a tree well tended. And now, nineteen years after that unforgettable incident, it looked as though the moment had finally come for the two of them to meet in mortal combat.

Her fingers closed tightly around the handle of the paper-knife. She smiled to herself. 'I'm ready for you!' she vowed grimly.

*   *   *

Craig glanced up and smiled at her as she walked into the boardroom. A smile, Fiona decided, that had much in common with the smile of a crocodile sizing up its lunch.

Well, you're wrong about that. Fiona looked him in the eye, as, returning his smile briefly, she seated herself opposite him. I have no intention of being anybody's lunch!

'I'm afraid Hamish is tied up. We'll conduct the meeting without him.' As he spoke, Craig flicked open one of the buff-coloured files that lay in a pile on the table in front of him, and Fiona was aware of a flicker of relief that Hamish, at least, was otherwise occupied.

She glanced across at Craig and was struck, as always, by how physically different he was from his brother. Hamish was shorter, much less powerfully built and had none of his older brother's striking presence. He was a mere worm to Craig's lethal viper.

The viper was addressing himself now to Sheena, Hamish's secretary, who sat in her customary discreet position, poised to take notes of the proceedings. 'Ready when you are,' he smiled across at her.

As Sheena nodded, he drew a sheaf of papers from the file and tossed them on to the table in front of him. 'I've been glancing through the minutes of your last progress meeting...' He paused and raised his eyes in Fiona's direction. 'I'm interested in this proposal of yours about opening up a chain of shops under the Birnam Wood name.'

Fiona glanced across at him. 'You don't find it madcap? I believe that was the word you used to describe my ideas.'

'Yes, it was.' Craig's expression never altered. The dark eyes fixed her across the table, rock-steady, hard, silently warning. He leaned forward, resting his forearms on the table. 'But this one struck me as potentially interesting. Why don't you tell me something about it?'

In spite of the apparently straightforward invitation, Fiona looked back at him with suspicion. What was he up to? What trickery was he intending? She'd be a fool if she imagined the invitation was what it seemed.

She sat back in her seat, widening the distance between them, and smoothed the skirt of her violet cashmere dress over her knees. 'It's a simple enough idea. I think we should open a few shops that sell only Birnam Wood furniture. At the moment, as you know, our main outlets are the big stores who sell our products alongside dozens of others.'

'Don't you think that's a perfectly satisfactory arrangement? After all, it's worked well for over thirty years.'

'I realise that, and I'm not suggesting that we should pull our products out of the big stores. But I tend to feel there's going to be a trend, as we move towards the twenty-first century, for people to prefer shopping in small specialist shops. I think it's a trend we ought to anticipate.'

Craig seemed to think about that. 'So, what have you done about it? Have you taken the proposal any further since it was discussed at the last meeting?'

Fiona frowned across at him. 'Of course I haven't! What on earth would be the point?'

He frowned back at her. 'You mean to say you've just been sitting on the idea? You haven't bothered to initiate the extensive market research programme that would necessarily have to precede such a venture? Isn't that a little unprofessional on your part?'

As Fiona looked back at him, she could feel her heart beating. An uneasy tension began to take hold of her. Either Craig had taken leave of his senses or else something very peculiar was going on.

She took a deep breath and leaned towards him. 'Why would I bother to go to all that trouble, when, as you would already know, if you'd read the minutes properly, Hamish vetoed the idea at our last meeting?'

'Vetoed the idea? Not according to the minutes I have.' Craig threw her a harsh look as he flicked quickly through the stapled pages and proceeded to quote in measured glacial tones, ' "The meeting ended with the proposal that Miss MacGregor should look more thoroughly into her proposition regarding the opening of specialist shops. She agreed to produce a rough market research questionnaire in time for the next meeting." '

Contemptuously, he tossed the pages aside, glanced up and fixed her with eyes like skewers. 'To me that does not sound like a veto.'

Numb with disbelief, Fiona was flicking through her own copy of the minutes of the previous meeting. And there they were, in indisputable black and white, the very words that Craig had just finished reading.

She swallowed numbly. 'I can't understand it. That isn't what happened. These minutes are wrong.'

'Wrong?' Craig raised a disbelieving eyebrow. 'How could they possibly be wrong?'

'I don't know. But they *are* wrong. That isn't what happened.' She had a sudden flash of inspiration. 'Somebody...somebody must have changed them.'

Craig responded with an almost pitying look, yet laced with a barely disguised contempt. 'Who would do that...and why?' he demanded impatiently. Then he paused and smiled a dagger-like smile. 'Let's ask Sheena about it, shall we? After all, it was she who wrote up the minutes. If anyone should know whether or not they've been changed, Sheena should, don't you agree?'

Fiona did not answer. In a sudden flash of insight she knew, before Craig had even invited her to speak, exactly what the secretary was going to say.

And she was absolutely right. Sheena shook her head and assured Craig, 'The minutes are exactly as I typed them. Nothing whatsoever has been changed.'

'You see! No dastardly alterations have been secretly made behind your back.' Craig's tone was clipped and sharp with impatience. 'So, I'm afraid you're going to have to find another excuse for your own lamentable lack of professionalism. What's the good of your having the occasional good idea if you're too damned lazy to follow it through?'

Suddenly the room had shifted out of focus. Just for a moment, Fiona was lost for words. And it was as she sat there struggling to make some sense of the madness that suddenly seemed to surround and engulf her that the suspicion suddenly struck her that this was a set-up.

The records had been deliberately doctored in order to make her look like an incompetent idiot.

And more than that, she sensed with a shiver. The ruse had been calculated to unnerve her. To confuse her, to cause her to call into question the soundness of her own intellectual faculties. For there had been a moment back there, as the room swam around her, when she had genuinely wondered if she might not be mistaken.

But she would not allow Craig's evil little game to upset her quite so easily. If he expected her to give way to anger and hysteria and tearful accusations that he had framed her, he was in for a cruel disappointment. He would discover she was not quite so easily unhinged.

In a tone whose coolness impressed even herself, she said, 'I apologise. There appears to have been a most unfortunate misunderstanding. I shall start pushing forward with the idea immediately. With any luck, I should manage to have a rough questionnaire ready for you by the end of the week.'

She smiled a deliberately sarcastic smile and added, 'I'm so pleased that, after all, the idea is considered worth pursuing.'

The expression on Craig's face had not softened in the slightest. No hint of an acknowledgement that she had sussed him. He looked right through her. 'Shall we move on to other business?' What, she wondered, was he plotting next?

The meeting proceeded smoothly and with satisfying speed. With any luck, Fiona was thinking, she would manage to grab an hour to get started on the market research programme this afternoon.

Then Craig reminded her, 'That conference-centre contract that was discussed at last week's meeting ... Have you made any progress there?'

Fiona nodded. 'Yes, I have.' As she reached into her file, she caught the cool, cynical look that passed across Craig's face. Was he expecting her, she wondered, to make a fool of herself again? He was in for a disappointment if he was. The facts and figures she was about to recite, she knew for sure, had not been doctored. They had been kept locked in her private drawer since she had first put them together earlier in the week.

She took a deep breath and regarded him confidently. 'I trust you're aware of the contract in question?'

He nodded. 'I'm aware of it, but I don't know the details. Perhaps you'd be good enough to fill me in?'

'Gladly.' She sat up straight. She was proud of this contract. It had been something of a personal coup. 'As you no doubt know, the big new conference centre in Glasgow is currently approaching completion. It's a substantial project, incorporating a number of conference rooms, plus accommodation for a couple of hundred people.' She paused before adding with a triumphant little flourish, 'And Birnam Wood Quality Repro, I'm delighted to say, have been invited to supply all the furniture!'

'Well done.' Craig smiled. 'Please remind me...which range of furniture did they choose?'

'They chose the Jacobean.' She flicked through the file. 'I've worked out some figures. Shall I just quickly run through them?'

'By all means.' Craig leaned back expectantly in his chair. 'We may as well end the meeting on a positive note.'

Fiona slid the sheet of figures from her file, laid it carefully on the table before her, and with just the tiniest hint of complacency began to recite the sums involved in the contract. At the start of this meeting she had been made to appear incompetent. Let anyone dare to level such an accusation now! This contract was one of the biggest orders the company had ever landed.

It was hard to say what set the alarm bell ringing in her head. It might have been the frown that from the corner of her eye she saw slowly settling on Craig's face, but, more probably, it was simply her own rapidly growing awareness, that seemed to freeze her insides with a suffocating sense of horror, that the figures she was quoting were horribly wrong.

She broke off in mid-stream and fumbled through her file. What was happening? Was she quoting from the wrong set of figures? But she had already worked out the nature of the disaster, as Craig put to her in a tone as rough as crushed granite,

'Forgive me, but, from my limited knowledge of prices, I would say that you appear to have given our clients a quite unprecedented discount... Either that, or the figures you're quoting are the wrong figures.'

Fiona felt as though her blood had turned to lead in her veins. She shivered as a wave of nausea clutched at her. She dared not look at him. 'They're the wrong figures,' she mumbled, anxiously tucking a strand of hair behind her ear.

'Then may we have the correct ones?' The demand cut like a whiplash. 'I can assure you I have better things to do than sit here and listen to a load of meaningless figures.'

'I'm afraid I can't.' She felt like dying. She prayed that the ground might open up and swallow her.

'Can't?'

'I'm afraid not.'

'Why?'

'I don't have them.'

'Then go and get them and stop wasting my time.'

If only she could! 'I can't. I don't have them. These are the only figures I have.'

There was a momentary silence that seemed to devour her. 'Would you kindly explain what you mean?'

Fiona took a deep breath. 'I don't know how it could have happened, but these figures...' She glanced down in sheer misery at the sheet of paper. 'These figures I've worked out are not for

Jacobean. I realise now they're for Chinese Chippendale.'

'Chinese Chippendale?' Craig's tone was devoid of mercy. 'I thought you said the order was for Jacobean?'

'It is.'

'I see.' His tone would have cut granite. 'The order is for Jacobean and you've worked out the figures for Chinese Chippendale.' As she dared to glance up at him, he narrowed his dark eyes at her. 'Have these figures been tendered to our client?'

Quite involuntarily, Fiona's fingers clutched at the table-edge. Any minute now, she thought, I'm going to throw up. Her stomach was churning like a cement-mixer inside her.

'I asked my secretary to fax the figures to them this morning.' She fell back in her seat, all her strength suddenly leaving her. 'Oh, lord,' she moaned, 'how could such a thing have happened?'

'That's precisely what I'm wondering.' With an angry gesture, Craig pushed back his chair and rose to his feet. He stood towering over her. 'Just don't try telling me that someone's mysteriously changed the figures. I warn you, it would not be wise to try that excuse twice!'

'I wasn't planning to.' Fiona stared at her twisting fingers. 'The figures are mine. I just don't know how it happened.'

'Don't you? Well, let me tell you something *I* don't know...!' He paused deliberately, willing her to look up at him. Then when she did, her cheeks ashen, he slowly continued, biting each word at her, grinding her to nothing, 'What I don't know is what someone capable of such gross incompetence is doing in a position of seniority in Birnam Wood Repro.'

His eyes flayed her face. 'It's a good job I came up here. I would say it's about time that some changes were made.'

CHAPTER THREE

BY A mere fluke disaster was averted, and the mind-boggling tens of thousands of pounds that Fiona's mistake might have cost the company were saved just in the nick of time.

For the first time in her life Fiona found herself indebted to a simple, but well-timed, technical failure.

After the disastrous progress meeting with Craig, once he had stormed in a black fury out of the boardroom, leaving Fiona hunched in her seat in a mortified heap, she had somehow found the strength to drag herself along the corridor to her secretary's office.

Grey-faced with despair, she stood in the doorway. 'Carrie... That fax I asked you to send off this morning...' She swallowed drily. 'I suppose it's gone?'

Carrie pulled a face. 'Oh, Miss MacGregor, I should have told you... The fax machine broke down this morning. The technician promised to come before lunchtime, but he's only just this minute gone. But, don't worry,' she added with a bright smile, reaching for the sheaf of papers on her desk. 'I'm just about to send it off now.'

Fiona dived across the room and had to restrain herself from snatching the sheaf of papers from the girl's hand. Light-headed with relief, scarcely believing her good luck, quite unable to stop the grin that spread across her face, she responded in a remarkably calm-sounding voice, 'That's just as well. I have some adjustments to make. We won't be able to send this off until tomorrow.'

Then, clutching the papers to her heaving bosom, she almost ran the short distance to her own office, snatched up the phone and instantly called Craig.

'It's all right,' she told him breathlessly when he answered. 'The figures haven't been faxed yet. I have them here. I'm going to get to work on the correct figures right away. It shouldn't take me more than a couple of hours at most.'

'Have them ready by five, then bring them along to me.' There was not a shadow of a hint that he was pleased to hear her news. His tone was as harsh and condemning as ever. 'I'd like to check them over before you fax them,' he added.

'That really won't be necessary.' She resented this intrusion. 'I made a perfectly straightforward mistake and I can assure you I'm quite capable of putting it right.'

'In that case, you have nothing to worry about, do you?' His response was laced with crushing sarcasm. 'But, just in case,' he added meaningfully, 'you should happen to make another straightforward mistake, I'm afraid I must insist on checking the new figures.

'By five!' he reiterated, before she could answer. 'In my office. I'll be waiting for you.'

Damn him! As he hung up on her, Fiona slammed the phone down. He was doing this deliberately, in order to humiliate her!

And yet, she thought ruefully, as she turned to her computer and punched in the command for the set of prices she needed, in a way she could scarcely blame him. That really was one corker of a mistake she had made, and she had no one to blame it on but herself.

Something squeezed inside her. That wasn't strictly true, for she remembered now the unpleasant incident that had caused her to make the fatal error.

An image of Hamish loomed up in her mind, causing her to shiver slightly. She had acknowledged that the problem she was having with Hamish was one that she didn't quite know how to handle, but she'd had no idea it was affecting her so deeply, to the extent that she could start making mistakes with her work.

That was worrying. She frowned at the screen of figures. Her work was one of the most important things in her life. She took an enormous pride in it and it mattered to her greatly that she should do, and be seen to be doing, a good job.

That business of the doctored minutes aside, she'd made a disastrous impression as regarded her professional capabilities, and at a time when it was vitally important that she do the very opposite. Craig, quite clearly, had already been regaled with a barrage of false tales about her incompetence, and was now simply looking for any excuse to get rid of her. Even if he had to invent it.

Fiona bit her lip. And she was playing straight into his hands, handing him on a plate, ready-made, the very ammunition he needed to destroy her!

She bent her head to the computer and glanced quickly at her watch. She would have the figures he had asked for, complete and double-checked for accuracy, on his desk, as he had commanded, by five o'clock!

'Come in and sit down.' As Fiona hovered in the doorway, Craig waved a hand towards the chair beside his desk.

She shook her head stiffly. 'That won't be necessary. I have the revised figures here...' She stepped quickly towards him and laid the pile of papers on the edge of his desk. 'I think you'll find they're self-explanatory.'

'Thank you.' There was not a shadow of a smile on his face, but his expression had softened since their last encounter. As she began to turn away again, he stood up and caught her arm. 'Don't be in such a hurry. I think we ought to have a chat.' He raised one dark eyebrow. 'Unless, of course, it's not convenient?'

His hand on her arm had caused her heart to skitter. It seemed at once too intimate, too possessive, too threatening. Fiona froze in mid-stride and forced herself to look at him with eyes that gave no hint of how much the physical contact bothered her. She would not give him that satisfaction.

She said, 'Unless it's terribly urgent, I think I'd prefer to have a little chat some other time. Besides,' she added, glancing down at the sheets of figures, 'I imagine you're anxious to start checking those.'

'They can wait until this evening. I'll take them home with me. I'm sure they'll make perfect bedtime reading.'

As he spoke, he released her and slipped his hands into his trouser pockets. 'Just an hour or so of your time; that's all I'm asking. I think it would be a good idea.'

A good idea for whom? Fiona regarded him suspiciously, wondering what was on that clever, devious mind of his. 'An hour or so? It sounds pretty heavy. What could we possibly find to say to one another for a whole hour?'

He smiled then, surprising her, causing the strangest sensation, as though two decades of her lifetime had suddenly fallen away. She had forgotten that, once, before she had grown to know him better, she had found that candid smile of his both exciting and beguiling. She had forgotten there had been a time when she had not disliked him.

She found herself taking a step back away from him as, that devious smile of his still dancing in his eyes, he put to her, 'Surely, after so long, we should have plenty to talk about? After all, it's years since we had a chat.'

He made it sound as though they had once been bosom buddies, this man who had brought pain and humiliation to her childhood and a sense of alienation that had taken her years to shake off!

She fixed him with a cold eye. 'What a cosy proposal. However, I can't say I'm in the mood for a friendly little chat.'

'In that case, we can simply stick to business.' As she started to turn away from him, once more he caught her arm. Only this time his grip was firm, uncompromising. With a flick of his wrist, he had twisted her round to face him. 'Either way, I must insist on having an hour of your time.'

'So I see.' Fiona narrowed her eyes at him, then lowered her gaze pointedly to her imprisoned arm. 'Kindly let go of me,' she commanded tightly. 'I'm not in the habit of being handled by bullies like you!'

Craig smiled again, but it was a cool, dismissive smile. 'No one would dare, would they? Bully you, I mean.' And still his fingers remained clamped around her arm. 'You're likely to lash out with that nasty, vicious tongue of yours. Much more effective than clubs or fists.' He smiled a strange smile. 'But that tactic won't work with me. I warn you, I'm immune to your nastiness.'

As he released her, Fiona frowned at him. What the devil had all that been about? Where had those ludicrous accusations come from? She'd had every right to call him a bully!

She narrowed her eyes at him. 'Is that so? Well, quite frankly, I really don't give a damn what you may or may not be immune to!'

Craig smiled a damning smile. 'I was wrong; you haven't changed. Behind that beautiful exterior, you really still are just as nasty as ever.'

Fiona tilted her chin at him, surprised at how his words had hurt her. She had believed he no longer had that power. It was an unpleasant shock to realise that he had.

'If I am nasty, I assure you, you can take all the credit. You taught me how when I was still very young.'

A frown narrowed his eyes a moment, then he slowly shook his head. 'No, I fear that particular skill came naturally. I wouldn't presume to take any credit.' He snapped up his wrist and glanced quickly at his watch. 'Let's not waste any more time. Go and get your coat.'

'My coat? What for?' Fiona looked back at him blankly. 'I had no idea we were going somewhere.'

'We're going to have that little chat I mentioned.' He smiled sarcastically. 'Had you forgotten already?'

'No, as a matter of fact, I hadn't.' Fiona pursed her lips angrily. 'But I was under the impression we were going to have it here.'

'Well, we're not. I've had enough of the office for one day. We're going out—we'll have to take your car, I'm afraid. I haven't got myself fixed up with a set of wheels yet—and we're going to find a nice congenial pub and we're going to have our little chat there.'

'I'm afraid I can't agree.' She had no desire whatsoever to do anything even remotely congenial with Craig Campbell. 'If you want to talk to me, you can talk to me here.'

Craig sighed. 'Must you make an issue of everything? No wonder you drive my brother round the bend.' Without glancing at her, he reached for his briefcase on the floor, stuffed in the sheaf of papers with the new contract figures, then strode past her to the cupboard where his coat was hanging, pulled it from its hanger and proceeded to slip it on.

He slid her an amused glance. 'If you insist on sulking, we can always have that chat tomorrow. Come to think of it, that might be better. Then Hamish can join us.'

That did it. The thought of Hamish sent a cold shiver through her. The last thing she wanted was an enforced meeting with him. These days she was finding it increasingly more difficult to look the wretched man in the eye.

She glanced at Craig. With Craig she did not have that problem. There was nothing at all complicated about her emotions for Craig. What she felt for Craig was clean, uncluttered hate.

With a resigned shrug, she swept past him. 'I'll go and get my coat. I'll see you outside in the car park.'

'You don't mind me driving?' Fiona threw him a mocking look as she snapped shut her seatbelt and switched on the engine.

'Not in the slightest.' Craig was pushing back the passenger seat to allow him to stretch his long legs more comfortably. 'Why on earth should I mind you driving? I presume you're perfectly competent at the wheel.'

The compliment surprised her and so did his attitude—and, if she were honest, it also irked her a little. She had expected him to suggest, if not to try to demand, as she led him across the car park to her shiny red Renault, that he be the one to take the driver's seat. It would have given her enormous pleasure to say no.

As she slipped into gear, she threw him a quick look. 'A lot of men object to being driven by a woman. They seem to think it——'

'Diminishes their masculinity?' Craig finished the sentence for her as she hesitated for an instant, uncertain of how most succinctly to put it. She felt him smile. 'That's their problem, isn't it? Personally, I don't feel my masculinity's that fragile.'

No, he wouldn't, would he? She might have known that. But, though she managed a cynical smile in response, Fiona was grateful for the dark interior of the car. Ridiculously, his words had brought a blush to her cheeks.

They were silent for a moment as she moved out on to the narrow road, banded on both sides by piles of fresh snow. The road itself was clear, the constant traffic had cleared it, though it glistened ominously in places, a warning of ice.

'Where do you fancy going?' She kept her eyes fixed to the front, as the snowflakes swirled and spun in the light of the headlamps. 'Did you have any particular pub in mind?'

'I thought about the Fair Maid. It's a cosy sort of place. Unless you have any other preference of your own?'

'The Fair Maid's fine.' Inwardly, she felt grateful. As Craig had said, it was a cosy little place, and it also had the advantage of being fairly close by. To be honest, she didn't particularly enjoy driving in this weather.

They were almost there, winding their way slowly along the twisting, tree-lined country roads, the trees stretching skywards like tall white ghosts, when Craig suddenly took her by surprise.

'Were you speaking from personal experience,' he enquired casually, 'when you spoke about some men feeling emasculated by the experience of being driven by a woman?'

Without thinking, Fiona jerked her head round to look at him, but in the darkness she found it hard to make out his features. 'What a peculiar question!' His eyes seemed to glint at her. 'Whatever gave you that idea?'

'Just a thought. You said it with such passion. So, I'm wrong, then?' he amended. 'The men in your life don't suffer such doubts about their masculinity?'

Again Fiona spun round. 'What business is it of y——?' But she never actually managed to finish the sentence, as in that very same instant the car hit an ice-patch, causing it to slew off to one side.

Instantly, Craig's hand was on the steering-wheel. 'Don't touch the brakes!' he commanded brusquely, as he pulled the car back into line.

Fiona pushed his hand away, doubly annoyed with him. 'I know how to drive on ice!' she shot back at him. 'I know it's lethal to slam on the brakes!'

To her annoyance Craig smiled. 'I'd say it's even more lethal to make innocent enquiries about your boyfriends.' He sat back in his seat. 'I won't say another word. Just forget that I'm here and tell me when we've arrived.'

Fiona cursed him in silence. Innocent enquiries! What a nerve he had to go prying into her private life. And with such an utterly gross lack of subtlety!

At last they drew up outside the Fair Maid.

'We're here.' Fiona snapped him a sideways look, as she unbuckled her seatbelt and switched off the headlamps. Then she pushed open the door and stepped outside, her boots crunching softly on the freshly fallen snow. She turned up the collar of her cashmere camel coat and shoved her hands deep into her pockets. 'It's cold,' she muttered. 'Let's go inside.'

But, as he joined her in the snow, Craig paused for a moment and glanced up at the sky, heavy with snow-clouds. 'I hope it keeps coming,' he murmured, almost to himself. 'I'd like to get some skiing in while I'm up here.'

Fiona glanced at his upturned profile, etched against the night—the straight, proud nose, the square, jutting chin, and those long black eyelashes, flecked now with snowflakes. Selfish swine, she thought. All he cares about is himself.

'Most people would prefer a bit less snow.' Her tone was as frosty as the ground beneath them. 'It's cruel and it's dangerous. People die in this cold weather. But then I wouldn't expect you to concern yourself with that.'

He glanced down at her then. 'For one so fallible you don't half have a high opinion of yourself. You pass down judgement like some goddess of Olympia.' He paused as, very slowly, a hard, humourless smile began to uncurl at the corners of his mouth. His hand touched her arm, guiding her to the pub entrance. 'I have a feeling I'm going to enjoy our little chat rather more than I'd expected.'

It didn't take an Einstein to work out what he meant by that. The purpose of their little chat, Fiona decided, fighting the nervous clench inside her, quite clearly was to stick a knife into her back.

The inside of the pub was warm and welcoming. A huge log fire burned in the grate, flickering and dancing and casting moving shadows over the clustered oak tables and their occupants. Craig found them a quiet table in a corner, ordered a whisky for himself and a Cinzano and soda for Fiona.

'It's years since I've been in here, but it's hardly changed at all.' As he slipped off his coat, he glanced around him. 'In the old days I used to come here a lot.'

'Did you really?' Fiona's tone was flat and hostile. She was interested in his habits neither past nor present, yet she was reluctant to move the conversation on to what they were here for. Unlike Craig, she had the feeling she was not going to enjoy it.

Craig laid his coat on the chair beside him. 'Are you sure you don't want to put your coat here, too? It's pretty warm in here. I'm sure you won't need it.'

Fiona had unbuttoned her coat but had no desire to shed it. That might look as though she intended staying, and she had no intention of staying a minute longer than need be.

She sat back in her chair as the barman brought their drinks. 'Where are you staying?' she enquired without interest. 'Are you staying with Hamish and Doreen?'

'Yes and no.' He took a mouthful of his whisky. 'I'm staying in what used to be the old granny house, down at the bottom of the garden. Remember, we all used to play in it as kids? It means I'm not under Doreen's feet all the time, although I shall probably have the occasional meal with them.'

Almost in spite of herself, Fiona smiled. She remembered the Campbells' old granny house well, and those long-ago visits she had made when they were all children. Though it was Hamish mostly she had played with in the granny house. Craig, six years older than herself, had been too grown-up to join in.

And as always the memories that came rushing back to her were a bewildering mixture of happy and hurtful. And, as always, it was the hurtful ones that stood out.

She picked up her glass and swirled the ice cubes thoughtfully, pushing those foolish, childish hurts away. Without looking at him, she observed, 'I was always rather surprised at the way you so generously handed over that gorgeous old house to your brother and his wife. After all, it was you your father left it to. I would have thought you would have wanted to keep it for yourself.'

'It's not much use to me when I spend most of my time in London.'

'No, but one day you might want to move back north.'

She said it without believing it. He would never move back. He'd left Inverairnie at the age of eighteen and made his first million by the age of twenty-five. Inverairnie and the old house meant nothing to him now.

'Who knows? I might.' He smiled amusedly as he said it. 'In the meantime, I've done up the granny house to suit me. It's perfectly adequate for my needs. Besides . . .' he caught her eye and regarded her obliquely '. . . if I decide I want the house back, I can always throw Hamish out.'

'You'd never do that.' Fiona threw him a shrewd look. 'Anyone else, you'd do it without batting an eyelid. But your beloved younger brother could burn the place down and you'd simply pay for it to be rebuilt and move him back in again.'

'You think so?'

'I know so. For you, Hamish can do no wrong.'

'He *is* my brother. My only brother. Why should I behave any differently?'

Fiona could have offered a thousand different reasons, but what would be the point when the plain truth was that Craig himself was just as bad as Hamish? Worse, she reminded herself. Much, much worse. Hamish was the worm to Craig's vicious viper.

At that very moment the viper chose to show his fangs. Craig sat back in his seat and looked directly across at her. 'I think we've had quite enough polite conversation.' He laid down his glass and smiled at her coldly.

'I suggest we drop the social niceties and get on with the subject we've come here to discuss.'

CHAPTER FOUR

FIONA swallowed the lump of fear in her throat and looked back at him without a flicker.

'Let's,' she agreed. 'I hate wasting time.' She even managed a sort of smile as she added, 'I'm sure we're both anxious to get home for supper.'

'Indeed.' Craig nodded. But there was something in his eyes that suggested that he feared that by the time he was through with her she wouldn't be feeling much like eating.

He reached for his glass and held it without drinking. 'You said you've been working with the firm for four years?'

'That's right.' Fiona nodded. So he was going to attack her obliquely, sidle up alongside her, then strike when she least expected it. Just to irritate him, she elaborated, 'I started when I finished college, in a very junior position in Sales and Marketing.' She held his eye. 'That's always been the area that's most interested me.'

'I see. And is that the only department you have experience in?'

'Oh, no.' She reached for her Cinzano and took a mouthful. 'My father always said that it was vitally important for anyone hoping to hold a senior position in any company to have a spell of working in all the various departments . . .'

As she paused, Craig nodded. 'Sound advice.' He smiled. 'But then your father always was a man worth listening to.'

At the easy words of praise, Fiona felt her fingers tighten with a stab of emotion round her glass. The praise was probably sincere. After all, Craig and her father had always got on exceedingly well. And that still irked her. Her father had been a smart man, but for some reason he had totally failed to see what a nasty piece of work Craig was beneath all the charm.

But the real cause now of the sudden tension in her was the memory of the cruel and vicious way that Craig had tried to drive a wedge of distrust between Fiona and her father. He had failed, but not through any lack of trying.

She pulled herself together. 'In answer to your question, I did a stint in every department at Birnam Wood Repro. Accounts, Design, Personnel... I think it was a pretty thorough grounding.'

'I'm sure it was.' His tone was expressionless. 'And then you settled down to work in Sales and Marketing?'

'Yes.' If only she could read what he was thinking. But the look in his eyes was distant, unreadable. 'When old Mr Douglas retired two years ago, I was promoted in his place to head of the department.'

'Quite a responsibility.'

He said it equably, but Fiona could tell where he was leading. She looked straight back at him. 'I enjoy responsibility. I've never found it a burden, if that's what you're suggesting.'

His eyes were unblinking. 'Surely there are times when everyone finds their responsibilities burdensome?' He smiled a fleeting smile. 'It's only natural. Even I have moments when I would be more than happy to off-load some of my responsibilities.'

But he would not charm her with his cosy false confessions. He would not draw her into his web. Fiona sipped her drink and regarded him flatly. 'In that case, perhaps you're not cut out for your job.'

He smiled at the gall of her. 'Is that your impression?'

'Perhaps you've bitten off rather more than you can chew?'

They were playing a bitter game now and both of them knew it. By a fluke she had managed, temporarily, to draw him away from the path he was pursuing. But for how long would he allow her to divert him?

'Perhaps you ought to have stayed here at Birnam Wood Repro.' To annoy him she would spin the game out for as long as she could. 'Perhaps you ought to have been a little less ambitious. After all, one man can't conquer the whole world.'

He sat back a little and regarded her with interest. 'Is that what you think I'm trying to do?'

'Something like that. I think you're endlessly ambitious. You lust after power. You can't get enough of it. It's the only thing in the world that really matters to you. But then I always knew that. Even as a child.'

Craig said nothing for a moment. His eyes watched her closely. 'You must have been a very sharp-eyed child...'

'I was.'

'Or a very imaginative one,' he amended meaningfully.

'Sharp-eyed, I think.'

'Perhaps a little too much. Perhaps you saw more than was actually there.'

Before she could reply, he leaned towards her. 'But we're straying from the subject we came here to discuss. We shouldn't be talking about me, we should be talking about you.'

Fiona was almost glad to be pulled back into line again. For the first time ever in all the years she'd known him something inside her had suddenly longed to bring him face to face with his sins.

It had been that flippant, smug remark about her imagination that had sparked off the angry, resentful feelings inside her. Suddenly she had felt like throwing in his face a few of the home truths he was so good at avoiding. Then let him have the nerve to say it was all imagination!

But there would be no point. He would only deny them. And besides, all those long-ago slights no longer mattered. She'd survived them and grown beyond them, and their only value now was that the memory of them was a constant reminder of the unkind nature of the man she was dealing with.

Fiona looked him in the eye, as though in challenge. 'You're right; we have strayed from the subject. Do continue with what you were saying.'

Craig smiled, an odd smile, and seemed to watch her for a moment. Then he sat back in his chair, reached out for his glass and let his long, tanned fingers curl slowly round it. Still watching her, he lifted the glass to his lips, took a mouthful, seemed to savour it, then laid the glass down again.

'We were talking about your job,' he continued at last, 'and the fact that the responsibility of it appears to be a little too much for you.'

'Is that what we were talking about?' Fiona's tone was sharp. 'I wasn't aware the conversation had progressed quite so far. I thought you were still speculating that I *might* find the job burdensome. I had no idea that it had been established that I did.'

'But you do, do you not?'

'Not in the slightest. I find it challenging and stimulating, but not in the least burdensome.'

'The evidence would suggest otherwise.'

Fiona leaned towards him. 'Are you trying to condemn me because of one mistake?'

Craig shook his head. 'Come, come,' he admonished. 'We both know there have been more mistakes than just one. Admittedly, I, personally, have only witnessed one, but I've been informed that that was just the latest of many.'

'I expect you have.'

'Meaning that you deny it?'

'I've told you already that I deny it, just as I've told you already that your brother's a liar.'

Craig sighed. 'If I had not been present at today's meeting and seen for myself that awful blunder over the prices, no doubt you would be insisting that that also never happened?'

'No, I wouldn't. *I'm* not a liar!' Fiona dropped her eyes from his for a moment. 'I'm not proud of that mistake I made. In fact, I'm horrified and ashamed.' She glanced up again, almost fiercely. 'I wouldn't go shouting it from the roof-tops, but neither would I be such a coward as to deny it.'

He was not even remotely impressed by her candour. 'Do you know something...?' He leaned towards her. 'If any employee in any of my companies were to make the sort of blunder that you made over those prices, regardless of whether it was their first mistake or not, I would fire them on the spot. I don't employ people to lose money for me.'

Fiona flinched visibly. His words were like a whiplash. Beneath his harsh gaze she felt her cheeks pale. From somewhere she found the strength to answer, 'Is that what you're proposing to do with me?'

He did not favour her with a direct answer. Instead, he lashed at her, 'At the very least, I would demote them to a position where they could do less damage.' He let the threat sink in, then he narrowed his eyes at her. 'Don't you think that would be a reasonable course of action?'

Fiona felt her stomach curl into a ball. A sick sensation went lurching through her. So, that was his strategy? He was planning to demote her. She was to be reduced to a cipher within the company.

She took a deep breath and felt a surge of anger replace the sense of dread that had settled inside her. 'I suppose I ought to have seen this coming,' she accused, 'right from the moment my father died.' As he frowned, she elaborated, 'While my father was alive, you would never have had the nerve to try to do this to me. But, now that he's gone, you find the way clear to edge me gradually out of the company. First demotion, then, no doubt, you'll find another excuse to kick me out altogether.'

Her cheeks were flushed with outrage as she leaned forward to challenge him, 'You never wanted me in the company! You think I don't belong! You've always thought that! Well, let me tell you what I've already told your brother... You're not going to get rid of me as easy as that!'

'And why would you tell my brother that? As I've already told you, he doesn't want rid of you.'

'Oh, but he does! I know he does! He's never actually said so in so many words, but he makes it very plain all the same!'

Craig shook his head impatiently. 'Why do you insist on lying? Why do you insist on trying to make out that you're some kind of victim? I happen to know that Hamish doesn't want rid of you. As a matter of fact, he doesn't even want you demoted. He spent an hour with me this afternoon, trying to persuade me to be lenient.'

'Hamish? You're joking?' She could not believe it.

'Why should I be joking? I find none of this funny.'

'Well, I do!' Fiona laughed dismissively. 'Do you seriously expect me to believe that Hamish defended me?'

'Believe what you like.' As he spoke, Craig eyed her narrowly. 'But the fact is that my brother would have me believe, in spite of all the evidence to the contrary, that you're doing your best and that you might even be getting better.'

This time, as she looked back at him, the laughter froze in her throat. Why was he going to the trouble to invent such crazy lies? Hamish, she knew, would never defend her.

Her heart skidded inside her. Was Craig trying to bamboozle her? Was this another of his ploys to confuse and disorientate her and thereby increase his control of the situation?

Yes, she decided, that sounded familiar.

But she would not be disorientated. She would not be bamboozled. She took a deep breath, feeling that streak of iron in her, that had brought her through the bad days of her childhood, straighten her spine now and stiffen her resolve.

'I'm not an incompetent, whatever you say,' she challenged him. 'I'm good at my job. And that blunder about the prices——'

'Never happened.' Craig's tone was caustic as he finished the sentence for her. 'That is what you were about to say, I take it?'

'As a matter of fact, it wasn't.' What she had been about to say was, That blunder about the prices happened because of your brother. But, as she looked now into Craig's disdainful, mocking face, she knew that to tell him the truth would get her nowhere. And in a way she was grateful that he had blocked her confession. It was unsavoury. Just to think of it made her shiver.

So she said instead, 'What I was about to say doesn't matter. What does matter is that you seem to think that because of one mistake you have the right to deprive me of my job. I can't let you do that. Not without a fight. My job means everything to me.'

'Not everything, surely? There must be more to your life than work?' He put the argument to her with a false, seductive smile, the dark eyes that held hers suddenly warm and intimate. 'With a less demanding job you would have more time to devote to other areas of your life. Your private life, for instance. That must suffer a little from the pressures that running the department put on you.'

'I haven't found so.' Fiona snapped her answer at him. As before when he had touched on the subject of her private life, she deeply resented the intrusion.

'Don't your boyfriends mind that you're always so busy? Wouldn't they prefer it if you had a little more free time?'

Fiona sat back in her seat and pulled her camel coat around her. Almost, she sensed, a protective gesture. But there was nothing defensive about her answer.

'Is that *your* problem, Craig?' she put to him in a cool tone. 'Don't you have enough time to keep your girlfriends happy?' When he didn't answer her, but simply smiled a knowing smile, she added in a tone that was stiff with resentment, 'Instead of wasting your time by coming up here and trying to play the heavy with me, you should have used the opportunity to spend a few days mollifying your neglected girlfriends.'

'You think they need mollifying?'

'I have no doubt that they do. As I've told you already, all you care about is business. The women in your life must have a horrible time—used like playthings for your occasional pleasure.'

To her annoyance he smiled. 'Only occasional? Do you see me as a man who takes his pleasures so rarely?'

It was the bold way he looked at her as he said it—she was absolutely certain that that was the reason—that caused her stomach to tighten like a snare drum. A vision of Craig engaged in fleshly pleasures flashed unbidden into her head, and the warm rush that went through her was startling and appalling.

She snatched her gaze away from him as he added, 'On the contrary, I hate to be without a woman for long. And I flatter myself, in spite of your suggestion, that I manage to keep the women in my life reasonably satisfied.'

Fiona flashed him a look then of purest condemnation. 'I'm afraid your personal habits don't interest me in the slightest.' Yet, even as she said it, the thought formed in her mind that he probably was pretty good at providing sexual satisfaction. She hated the way that thought sent another warm rush through her.

Angry with herself—was she taking leave of her senses?—Fiona forced herself to look back at him steadily. 'Well, why don't you go back, then, and satisfy them some more? Without delay? Tonight, for example?'

'You'd like that, wouldn't you?'

'I'd like nothing better.'

'Well, I'm afraid I'm going to have to disappoint you.' With a cold smile Craig drained the whisky in his glass. 'I shall be going back to London when my business here is finished.' He looked her in the eye. 'And it's barely started yet.'

'By business, you mean your campaign to drive me out?' She held his gaze and smiled a caustic smile. 'I apologise for my reluctance to make things easy for you. Perhaps you thought you could persuade me over a cosy little drink to step down for the sake of my supposedly imperilled social life?'

Pointedly, she pushed her half-empty glass aside and proceeded to button up her coat. 'Well, I'm sorry to disappoint you, but I really have no intention of giving up a job I thoroughly enjoy and that I happen to know I'm extremely good at.

'And now, if you don't mind...' she glanced quickly at her watch '...I'd like to get home. Iris will have dinner ready.'

Craig hadn't moved a muscle. He regarded her unblinkingly, an expression of thoughtful amusement in his eyes. 'So, you still have Iris? Quite the pampered lady, aren't you? I wouldn't have thought you'd need a live-in housekeeper now that you're on your own.'

Though it stuck in her gullet, Fiona ignored the criticism. There was no way she intended defending herself to him. How she chose to live her life was none of his damned business!

She looked back at him levelly. 'It's a big house,' she answered flatly.

'It is indeed. Do you need a house that size? Why don't you sell it and buy something smaller?'

'Because I like it where I am. Do you have any objections? Is there something about my living arrangements that bothers you?' she demanded crisply.

Craig's smile widened. 'Not in the slightest. I confess I was merely thinking of you. It must be a rather expensive house to run.' He paused a beat before continuing, and his smile seemed to sharpen with malice as he added, 'Perhaps, in the circumstances, you ought to be thinking of making slightly more economical arrangements.'

His words and the glint in his eyes that accompanied them sent a ripple of icy alarm rushing through her. What he had just issued was a barely disguised warning and a clear declaration that he definitely meant business. He might as well have told her in straightforward English that by the time he had finished with her she would no longer be able to afford the luxury of her current living arrangements.

Fiona's jaw tightened angrily as she glared back at him. 'Thanks for the advice. Your concern is most touching. But I really don't foresee the need for me to make any changes in my living arrangements.'

'Don't you?'

'No.'

'I admire your optimism.'

'Do you? How nice.' Her tone was brittle. 'I wish I could say that I saw something to admire in you. But I'm afraid I can't. Not one single thing.'

'Not even when you employ those legendary sharp eyes of yours?'

'Not even when I employ my even more legendary imagination.'

Their eyes locked and held across the bar table, the violet and the black, in stony, hostile silence.

Then Fiona rose to her feet. 'I told you, I'd like to leave now. Iris will be waiting with my dinner.'

'Go, then. I'm not stopping you.' Craig sat back in his seat. 'I think I'll stay and have another whisky.'

'How will you get home?' She asked the question without thinking, and instantly wished she hadn't as he smiled,

'Oh, I expect I'll manage to get a taxi. But it's decent of you to be concerned.'

'I wasn't concerned. Please don't think it for a minute.' She smiled a steely smile. 'I was just being polite.'

'Not like you at all.' He stood up slowly, picking up his empty glass from the table. And suddenly he seemed to be standing right over her, crowding her into the corner beside her chair.

Just for a millisecond, Fiona felt oddly trapped. She looked up into his face as a strange panic seized her, causing her heart to race and her hands to grow clammy.

Then, smiling, he stepped aside. 'You'd better be on your way, then. You don't want to keep Iris and your dinner waiting. I'll see you tomorrow,' he added as she darted past him. 'We can continue our little conversation then.'

Fiona turned to look at him, hating him in that moment more than she had ever hated him before. What he was trying to do to her meant absolutely nothing to him. The destruction of her life and her career moved him no more than the act of stepping on a bug.

Deep in his eyes, where there ought to have been regret and compassion, all that was visible was a careless disdain and, even more shocking, a shadow of amusement.

She met that amusement with a look of cold contempt. 'Thanks for the drink. And goodnight,' she told him crisply. Then she turned on her heel and headed briskly for the door.

His voice, with that maddening smile in it, followed her across the room. 'Goodnight. Drive safely. And remember what I told you...keep your foot off the brake if you hit a patch of ice.'

Fiona did not glance back at him and did not break her stride till the pub door slammed behind her and she stepped out into the snow. Then she paused for a moment, snowflakes swirling all around her, her hands thrust deep into the pockets of her coat, and forced herself to breathe deeply and slowly until the suffocating anger within her had subsided.

Then, once more calm and in control of her emotions, she headed towards her car across the drifting snow.

CHAPTER FIVE

BY A miracle Fiona made it home to Bonnie Braes in one piece.

It had required every single ounce of her will-power to keep her concentration fixed on the icy road and to stop it straying angrily away to the contemplation of how much she detested Craig Campbell.

She parked the car in the garage, then hurried up the path, across a carpet of deep, soft snow to the big red front door with its gleaming brasses. And as always, as she slid her key into the lock and stepped into the warm and welcoming hallway, with its deep crimson carpet and oak-panelled walls, she was aware of a soothing sense of well-being. A cosy, reassuring sense of being home.

Yet, as she slipped off her coat, Fiona found herself reflecting that, in the past, she had not always felt that reassurance. There had been a period in her life when she had felt a stranger in this house. An interloper. Thanks to Craig Campbell.

She shook the snow from her coat and was heading for the cloakroom when a stout, smiling figure appeared in the dining-room doorway.

'Miss MacGregor, you're home. I was just a wee bit worried at the thought of you driving home in this weather.'

Fiona smiled at the woman fondly. 'I'm glad to be back. It's nasty out there and it's getting nastier.'

'Never mind; just as soon as you're ready, I've got a lovely lamb casserole waiting in the oven for you. And a nice apple charlotte and custard for afters.'

'Sounds terrific. Just what I feel like.' Fiona smiled to herself as she hung her coat in the cloakroom, and reflected that, considering the deliciously hearty meals that Iris always insisted on feeding her, it was a blessing she wasn't prone to putting on weight!

She closed the cloakroom door. 'Just give me five minutes to change out of these boots and things and I'll be with you.'

'Take as long as you like, Miss MacGregor,' Iris nodded. 'I've got the heat down low. There's no danger of it spoiling.'

Fiona threw her a wink as she hurried upstairs and the plump homely figure retreated to the kitchen. Iris had been housekeeper to herself and her father since she was eight years old, just shortly after Elsa MacGregor, her adoptive mother, had tragically died. It was Iris, really, who had brought her up.

It was Iris who had helped her with her homework and dried her tears when she fell and skinned her knees. It was Iris who had explained to her the facts of life and who had reassured her with words full of love and common sense in those cold, dark days when she had felt so unwanted.

'Fiona,' she had told her, setting her on her knee and wrapping her ample arms around her, 'I don't know what those Campbell boys have been telling you, but I've never in my life heard such a heap of nonsense. Of course your father loves you. Of course he wants you. Don't you ever for one minute believe anything different.'

Fiona smiled now as she reached the top of the stairs and hurried down the corridor to her bedroom. In those days Iris had called her by her first name, but all of that had stopped on Fiona's fourteenth birthday.

'You're a young lady now,' Iris had insisted. 'It wouldn't be right me being so familiar.'

Fiona's protests had got her nowhere and over the years she had come to accept the rather more formal form of address. But the warmth between them had never diminished, and Fiona knew that deep in her big, warm heart Iris still secretly thought of her as simply 'Fiona'.

She kicked off her boots now and pulled her dress over her head, then hung the dress in the wardrobe and slipped on a loose kaftan. And to think that Craig Campbell had presumed to pass judgement on her relationship with Iris!

Anger drove through her. He thought Iris was just a servant. But he was wrong about that. Iris was a part of her life. And she would never part with her. Never! she vowed angrily. Not even if, as he had so callously predicted, she should find herself in financially reduced circumstances. She would sell the house and all her possessions before she would ever put Iris out on the street!

She paused before the full-length mirror as she slipped her feet into comfortable slippers, and gazed at her reflection for a long, thoughtful moment.

Would he really do that to her? she wondered, frowning. Would he really, seriously, try to edge her out of the company, with demotion the first crushing step in the process?

Yes, he would, her reflection silently answered. To edge you out is what he has always secretly wanted. So, be prepared for a merciless, no-holds-barred fight.

Her frown deepened as she remembered the battles of the past, battles she had fought alone and at times had come close to losing when the cruelties that had been hurled at her had become almost unbearable.

'Craig says you don't belong. You're not one of us,' Hamish, Craig's little mouthpiece, had been fond of telling her. 'And your father, who, of course, isn't your real father at all, never really wanted you. Craig says the MacGregors only adopted you out of pity,' he'd elaborated, as she'd fought back the tears. 'Your real mother wasn't even married and, when she died, nobody else wanted you.'

She knew that the story was, in part at least, true. Her natural mother, abandoned by the man she had loved, the uncaring father of her tiny infant daughter, had taken her own life in a fit of depression just a few short weeks after Fiona's birth. The MacGregors, still childless after twelve years of marriage, had adopted her when she was only six weeks old and brought her up as though she were their own. She knew these details because Iris had told her when one day, tearfully, she had confided her misery.

'Of course your father loves you,' Iris had reassured the weeping child, pressing her warmly against her ample bosom. 'Just as your mother loved you while she was alive.'

'But he never told me! He never told me I was adopted! And he never tells me that he loves me!'

Iris had smoothed back her hair and kissed her tear-stained face. 'That doesn't mean he doesn't,' she promised. 'He's a very busy man. He doesn't think to tell you. And, perhaps, these days, since Mrs MacGregor died, he's feeling a little sad himself. And I'm sure the only reason he didn't tell you you were adopted was because he didn't want to upset you ...'

'It's because he's ashamed of me! That's what Craig says!'

'Nonsense. It isn't.' Iris had looked at her almost fiercely. 'Don't ever think such a thing, Fiona. What man in his right mind could possibly be ashamed of a beautiful, clever little daughter like you?' Then she had hugged her close again. 'Stop thinking these things. And, above all, stop listening to these nasty Campbell boys.'

Fiona sighed now. What cruel times those had been. For though she'd listened to Iris and tried to believe her the doubts had remained inside her for years. It hadn't really been until her teenage years that she had finally realised the truth—that her father thought the world of her, and had always done so, and that he was proud that she should be his heir.

And now... She sighed and moved away from the mirror. The campaign of cruelty was starting all over again. Only this time Craig meant serious business and that was why he was personally taking the helm.

Her jaw firmed determinedly as she headed for the door. Well, this time he would find her a less fearful adversary. This time he would discover he had a real battle on his hands.

She was halfway down the stairs when she heard the phone ring, then stop abruptly as, through in the kitchen, Iris answered it. As Fiona crossed into the dining-room, Iris stuck her head round the door.

'That was Mr Campbell. Mr Craig Campbell,' she announced. 'He was asking if you'd got home safely.'

'How kind.' Fiona smiled grimly and observed to herself that this show of concern was like that of a cat who enjoyed keeping its prey alive, the longer to torment it. What a callous, deceitful, hateful man he was!

Then she smiled at Iris, shrugging off all thoughts of Craig. 'Bring on the lamb casserole. I'm absolutely starving!'

'You will come, won't you? We'll have dinner all together. All four of us, just like one big happy family.'

Fiona grimaced into the phone. The prospect appalled her. But her brain had gone dead. She couldn't think of an excuse.

'That's very kind of you, Doreen,' she responded sweetly. 'But wouldn't you rather have dinner with just the three of you? After all, I'm scarcely family, am I?'

'You're as good as family. And I insist that you join us.' Hamish's wife, Doreen, was absolutely adamant. 'I simply won't take no for an answer!'

'Then what can I say? I'd be delighted to join you. Thank you, Doreen. I look forward to it.'

With a deep sigh, Fiona laid down the phone. She had never uttered a more scandalous lie in her life!

'So, you'll be joining Hamish and Doreen and me, after all. I'm so pleased to hear it. It wouldn't be half so much fun without you.'

Fiona glanced up with a start to see Craig standing, in that arrogant way he had, in the doorway of her office.

She scowled at him in annoyance. 'Do you make a habit,' she demanded, 'of listening in to other people's conversations?'

'Not exactly a habit. But at times it can be interesting.' He straightened slowly and smiled with dry amusement. 'I must say you're quite a convincing little liar.'

'And you are a shameless, unprincipled eavesdropper!' This time, she could scarcely deny the allegation, so instead she retaliated with an insult for an insult.

But, as always, the insult bounced harmlessly off him. He stepped into the room and stood before her desk, pushing his hands into the pockets of his trousers. 'Why didn't you just tell Doreen you didn't want to join us for dinner? Wouldn't that have been more honest?'

'Possibly.' Fiona leaned back in her seat, instinctively widening the space between them. 'It would also have been just a little impolite, and, unlike you, I don't enjoy offending people.'

'Ah. I see.' His tone was mocking. 'I forgot, you're so sensitive to the feelings of others.' His mouth hardened at the corners. 'You're forgetting, surely, that I happen to have known you for a very long time, and sensitivity to the feelings of others is not a characteristic I remember.' He smiled a caustic smile. 'This new sensitive side to you must be a fairly recent development.'

Fiona frowned. What was he getting at? She felt genuinely bewildered, just as she had the other day, when he had made a similarly mysterious and cutting comment.

But she felt no great urge to ask him to explain himself. What did she care what Craig Campbell thought of her? His opinion of her could be no lower than hers of him.

She held his eyes a moment, then reached out disdainfully to pick up the uncapped pen on her desk. Then, feigning a total calmness she was really far from feeling—his arrival in her office could only mean trouble—she glanced down and began to doodle on her blotter.

'Is there some particular reason for this intrusion? Or were you just passing,' she demanded, glancing up, 'and couldn't resist the opportunity to come in and bother me?'

'Oh, there was a reason.' He smiled as he said it, one of those quick, callous smiles of his that could literally make her soul freeze. Then, to her dismay, he seated himself on the edge of her desk, folded his arms across his chest and swivelled round to look at her. His tone was quite emotionless as he continued, 'Unfortunately, we haven't had a chance to continue our little chat of the other evening. I was wondering if you'd had any further thoughts on the matter?'

'What kind of thoughts?' She looked up at him calmly, but her hand had frozen over the blotter. Suddenly, beneath the blue silk blouse she was wearing, her heart was pounding like a hammer.

'The sorts of thoughts I suggested.' His tone was steely. 'The sort of thoughts that would involve your taking a step or two down the ladder.'

Fiona looked back at him hard. 'No, I'm afraid I haven't.'

Craig continued to look down at her, unfolding his arms now, and reached out to pick up the Caithness paperweight that lay beside him on the desk. He seemed to weigh the heavy glass sphere in his hand as he put to her in a reasonable tone of voice, 'Naturally, you would retain your position on the board and could still draw the monthly dividend to which your share of the company entitles you. On that level things would remain as they are.'

'For the moment.' Fiona's voice felt tight in her throat. 'Until you could find a way to edge me out completely!'

Craig regarded her for a moment, his expression dark and shuttered, passing the paperweight from one hand to the other, his movements unhurried and intensely irritating.

'There is always that possibility, if you'd prefer it.' He raised one dark eyebrow at her and continued. 'If you feel you'd be happier out of the business altogether, then I'm sure we could come to some arrangement...'

'Arrangement?' All at once, her limbs were trembling. Her fingers that had frozen over the blotter were clenched into an angry fist. 'What kind of arrangement exactly are you suggesting?'

Craig smiled and glanced down at the paperweight in his hand, like a fortune-teller consulting a crystal ball. 'Well, the most simple solution, if you were to want out, would be for either me or Hamish to buy your share from you.' He smiled a glancing smile. 'More likely it would be me. Hamish might have a problem raising that amount of cash.'

Of course it would be him. She had never doubted that. He was the one who was always in control.

She looked back at him tightly. 'You'd have it all then, wouldn't you? The whole of the company, as near as damn it! Then Hamish could continue to run things for you, without any more tiresome opposition from me, and both of you would wind up happy.'

'All three of us, I'd say.' The paperweight glinted, as he continued to shift it from one hand to the other. 'You'd find yourself with a substantial sum of money that you could either use to live on or invest in something else. Something to which you were more suited. Something smaller, that would make fewer demands on you.'

'How very generous of you to take the time to give my interests such thoughtful consideration.' Fiona was so furious she felt she might choke on the words. How dared he have the gall to make such a suggestion?

But Craig's gall was boundless, as she ought to have realised. And so far she had only glimpsed the tip of the iceberg.

He laid down the paperweight and swivelled his eyes towards her, quite unmoved by the bitterness of her sarcasm. 'Surely it's only natural that I should consider your position? After all, your father and mine were partners and we've known each other since we were children.'

A cool smile touched his lips, a smile devoid of affection. 'We've never been close, but we go back a long way, and the length of our association, as I see it, imposes on me certain duties.' He smoothed the burgundy silk tie at his throat and glanced down at Fiona with a kind of mocking pity. 'One of these duties, in my opinion, is to ensure that you're well settled in the right career, a career that's appropriate to your capabilities.'

He paused before adding, 'And, quite clearly, at the moment, sadly, that is not the case.'

Fiona's fury was so overpowering that she could not remain seated. It smouldered, red-hot, like a volcano inside her, threatening to tear her apart if she did not release it.

She rose slowly to her feet, her whole body trembling, leaning her fists against the desk-top for support.

'You really are something! You really are incredible!' Her violet eyes blazed as she fired the words at him, each one a dagger tipped with poison. 'What makes you think you have the right to come here like some knight of old on a make-believe crusade to save a poor damsel in distress? What a hypocrite you are! What a shameless hypocrite! If you want to know, you make me sick!'

Something flickered in his eyes, almost a warning, then he smiled at her cynically. 'I'll say this for you—you really do have a most colourful turn of phrase. I'd never thought of myself as a knight of old. Even less have I ever considered myself to be on any kind of crusade. I fear you're letting your imagination run away with you again.'

The mockery in his voice was cruel and deliberate. It seemed to strike her like an open palm. Fiona caught her breath, hating him so fiercely that her hatred was like an object, real and substantial, that she could actually see and hold in her hand.

She breathed slowly for a moment, struggling to control herself, fearful of the power of the bubbling volcano that still wrenched and tore and battled inside her. Were she to release it, there was no knowing what damage it might do.

'You're the one who's allowing his imagination to run away with him if you think for one moment that there's the tiniest likelihood of my falling for this neat little plan you've cooked up!' She paused for breath. Her head was spinning. Her anger was so intense she could barely focus. 'If you think you can talk me into believing that you're doing me a favour by forcing me to step down, I can assure you you're living in cloud-cuckoo-land! I know you for what you are! I can see behind your mask! Doing people favours is not your strong point.' She laughed harshly. 'And certainly not when it comes to me!'

'Look at it this way, then, since you refuse to accept that I might actually be motivated by concern for your welfare...' He spoke the words slowly with the clipped precision of one who was rapidly losing patience. And at the back of his eyes the warning flashed again, as he continued, 'Instead of thinking of it as me trying to do you a favour, think of it as you doing a favour to yourself. Perhaps that more selfish viewpoint might appeal to you a little more?'

There was something quite unbearable about the arrogance in his eyes and the way he continued so coolly to sit there, so poised, so sure of himself, on the edge of her desk.

Fiona thrust her chin at him. 'Get off my desk this instant! Get off my desk and get out of my office!'

He did not move. He simply smiled amusedly. Make me, the look in his eyes seemed to say.

And it was in that instant, as Fiona glared back at him, that something inside her seemed to snap, dissolving in a flash her earlier grim resolve to keep her anger under control.

'I said get off my desk! Didn't you hear me?' She raised her fists threateningly, her eyes burning fiercely. 'If you won't get off, I'll have to remove you!'

He found her threats comical. He shook his head, smiling. 'And how do you intend to do that?' he challenged.

It was then, as the anger surged up inside her, like a kind of madness, uncontainable, that she leaned forward and tried to push him off the desk. Without success. It was like trying to move a mountain.

And suddenly the frustration was too much to bear. What had started as a push became something else, as, with a cry of rage Fiona leaned across the desk and began to lash out at him with her fists. And a crude sense of animal satisfaction rushed through her as she felt her bare knuckles make contact with his face.

Ebullient with triumph, she lunged at him again. 'You pig! Don't think you can still bully me!' she screeched. 'I'm not the meek little child I used to be, too in awe of you to try to stop you tormenting me!'

But this time, as she let fly with a vicious right hook, her arm was caught and pinioned in mid-air. Next instant Fiona found herself being hauled across the desk-top as a voice rough with anger growled into her ear, 'OK, if you want to get physical, let's get physical!'

CHAPTER SIX

'Is THAT what you want?' Craig snatched Fiona closer, so that she had to struggle to keep her balance. Her feet were barely touching the floor.

She gritted her teeth and glared at him defiantly, knowing that she had well and truly asked for this. Craig was not the type of man to stand by meekly and allow someone to punch him in the jaw, even if that someone happened to be a woman. And she had hit him rather hard, she realised with some pleasure, as she glanced at the red weal that had formed around the spot where her knuckles had made contact with the side of his face.

'Because if you do...intend to get physical...I'll be more than happy to oblige you.' His fingers tightened around her wrist as he growled at her, 'If you want a fight, Fiona, I'll be happy to give you one.'

'No doubt you would, you disgusting bully! Fighting women is probably the sort of thing you go in for. What a noble, courageous man you are!'

'I suppose you think that what you just did was noble and courageous? Striking someone whom you knew would not strike back?' His eyes bored into her. 'Yes. Very noble.'

'I didn't know you wouldn't strike back!' Her eyes flickered as she said it. The denial was untrue. She had known he would retaliate, but she had known also that he wouldn't strike her, and she had taken deliberate advantage of that.

Craig smiled. 'What a shameless little faker you are. Or do you actually believe all that rubbish you're for ever talking?'

He still held her by the wrist, she was still doubled across the desk. Fiona gave her arm a determined tug, vainly attempting to free herself. 'All what rubbish?' she demanded sharply.

'All that rubbish about your being some kind of victim. The poor innocent victim whom the whole world's after.'

'Not the whole world. Just you, Craig Campbell!' She had suddenly become conscious of his skin against her skin, of the warmth and the power of him, of his disconcerting closeness. It was years since she had felt so physically aware of him. And it was an awareness that made her feel sharply uncomfortable.

She jerked her hand roughly. 'Let me go!' she demanded.

But he did not let her go. Instead, he leaned a little closer, his face inches from her own, his dark eyes burning into her. 'And why am I after you? Kindly explain. What's behind this monstrous malice you perceive?'

That was easily answered. 'You hate me,' she shot back at him. 'You've always hated me. Don't try to deny it.'

Craig looked back at her in silence for a moment, and there was this much to say for him—he did not offer a denial. Instead, abruptly, he released her, rose slowly to his feet and stepped with an impatient gesture away from the desk. He pushed his hands into his trouser pockets and narrowed his eyes at her.

'Has it ever occured to you,' he put to her in a cool tone, 'that sometimes you make yourself extremely easy to hate?'

Fiona felt herself blanch at the crude hostility of that accusation. Though by now, she chastised herself, she ought to be used to such abuse.

'Oh, it was bound to be *my* fault!' Her tone was sarcastic. 'I might have known you'd claim that the only reason you hate me is because I deserve to be hated!'

'That isn't what I said.'

'Then I must have misheard you.'

'I reckon you must have.' Craig's tone was impatient. 'Or perhaps your hearing's like all your other faculties—subject to the vagaries of your overactive imagination.'

'So, we're back to that.' Fiona stood behind her desk, arms folded stiffly over her chest. Inside she was trembling with anger and resentment and an almost crippling sense of frustration. He twisted everything she said and threw it back at her, contemptuously, trying to put her in the wrong.

She glared at him. 'I told you to get out of my office.'

'Don't worry, I'm going.' Craig glanced at his watch. 'I have work to do and, no doubt, you have work to do, too.'

As he headed for the door, he turned suddenly and smiled at her. 'Don't forget dinner tonight.

Eight o'clock sharp. We'll all be looking forward to seeing you.'

Fiona did not answer. Frozen-faced, she glared back at him. She had not known it was possible to loathe someone quite as much as she loathed Craig Campbell at that moment.

If there had been any way of politely getting out of dinner that evening, Fiona would have done so without hesitation. Of all the people in the world, Craig, Hamish and Doreen were the three whose company she relished least—though, these days, the antipathy she felt for Doreen was mildly tempered by feelings of compassion. One could not help but feel a degree of pity, after all, for any woman cursed with a philandering husband.

The thought brought an image of Hamish into mind, accompanied simultaneously by a shudder of revulsion. She tried to push the feeling from her. It would only make the evening more difficult if she were to dwell on her recent unfortunate experiences with Hamish. And surely there was no danger of a recurrence this evening?

Hamish and Doreen lived on the other side of Inverairnie, in the magnificent, rambling old country manor house that had been bought and restored back in the fifties by old Fergus Campbell, Craig's and Hamish's late father. It stood on a hill, surrounded by woods and parkland, dominating the countryside for miles all around. And, in spite of some of the less than happy hours she had spent there, Fiona had always harboured a secret fondness for the place.

Like its former owner, old Fergus, it possessed a warmth and a natural dignity that even its new occupants couldn't erase. Though they had come close, Fiona mused, as she drove through the main gates illuminated by a pair of showy brass lanterns, and headed up the wide driveway, now laid with crazy paving, where before there had been simple old-fashioned gravel. A few more years in the hands of Hamish and Doreen and the place would be left with about as much dignity as a fun-fair.

Fiona parked her car at the front of the house and shivered as she stepped out into the icy night air. It was snowing again. It had been snowing for most of the day, and the air was so cold it was like breathing sharp knives.

She hated the winter, she decided, slamming the door shut and pulling the collar of her coat around her ears. She had always hated it. She longed for the summer. Yet it seemed appropriate somehow that this bitter, dead season should be the time of year that Craig should choose to implement his final plan against her.

With a small frown she plunged her hands into her pockets and headed across the snow to the front door. Where would she be when spring came? she wondered. Would she have won her battle, or lost it?

She pressed her finger firmly against the doorbell. If she lost it, it would not be for the lack of fighting. She intended to fight every inch of the way.

The door opened and Hamish was standing before her, beaming broadly, the warm, expansive host.

'Come in, come in. You look frozen to death.' He stood aside to let her pass into the hall, then quickly closed the door behind her. 'You're in perfect time. We're just about to have drinks.' He stepped towards her. 'Here, let me take your coat.'

'It's all right, I can manage.' Automatically, Fiona stepped away from him, as he reached out to help her off with her coat. Yet, she was aware all the same of his hand brushing against her body just a little more intimately than was strictly necessary.

She stepped aside quickly, anger throbbing through her. So, she was to be submitted, even here, to his sexual harassment, obliged to ward off yet another of his passes, despite the fact that his wife was probably in the next room!

She threw him a harsh look, the colour rising to her cheeks, as that familiar sensation of anxiety and revulsion rose up inside her like a tidal wave. 'Don't play those silly games with me. I've told you endlessly. Please don't make it necessary for me to tell you again.'

His pale eyes narrowed. He smiled a sly smile. 'It's not games, exactly, I have in mind. But, don't worry, this is neither the time nor the place. Pity.' He winked and subjected her to a lewd look. 'I'll wait until we're just a little more private.'

'Oh, you will, will you? Well, let me tell you something——!'

But she got no further, for at that moment a tall, commanding figure, dressed in an immaculate dark grey suit, appeared in the doorway of the drawing-room and paused there for a moment before stepping out into the hall.

'Good evening.' The remark was directed at Fiona. Craig took a mouthful from the glass in his hand. 'I see you made it. Is it still snowing outside?'

'Yes.' She felt oddly relieved to see him. The threat posed by Hamish seemed instantly to recede.

She heard Hamish say, 'I'll put your coat in the cloakroom, then I'll go and join Doreen in the kitchen. I think she could probably do with a hand. Craig, you look after Fiona for me, will you? Take her through to the drawing-room and fix her a drink.'

'My pleasure.' Craig had never for one second taken his eyes off her, and she likewise had kept her eyes fixed firmly on his face. It was funny, she mused, as he stood aside now to allow her to pass ahead of him into the drawing-room, how, the instant Craig had arrived on the scene Hamish seemed almost to become invisible.

It was a measure of the disparity in the sheer physical presence of the two brothers. And a reminder, if one was needed, of which one she ought to fear.

She walked ahead of him into the too brightly lit room with its ostentatiously expensive furnishings. How different it all was from the days of old Fergus, when it had been filled with comfortably mellow antiques, with a real log fire burning in the huge hearth instead of the fake gas monstrosity that was installed there now.

'What would you like to drink? Cinzano and soda?'

As Fiona seated herself on one of the over-stuffed sofas, Craig crossed to the bar and laid down his drink. She followed him with her eyes, acknowledging with some surprise that he had actually remembered what she had had to drink last night at the pub.

For that very reason, because he had got it right—for Cinzano and soda was her favourite tipple—she was deliberately contrary and shook her head. 'I'd rather, if you don't mind, have a Campari and soda.' Not even in so small and unimportant a matter was she prepared to let him have the psychological advantage. He might start to think he had her figured out!

'One Campari and soda coming up.' She could not see his expression as he quickly poured her drink, tossing ice and a wedge of lemon into the glass first, but she thought she could detect an amused note in his voice. Perhaps he had guessed that she'd been deliberately awkward and in his usual superior way simply found the gesture amusing.

He retrieved his own glass and came towards her, then paused for an instant, laying down both glasses, to quickly switch off one of the wall-lamps.

'That's better.' He came over and handed her her Campari, then seated himself on the sofa opposite her. 'I don't think that extra light is really necessary...that is, as long as neither of us is planning on subjecting the other to a third degree.'

He smiled as he said it, but Fiona did not smile back. She felt irritated that he should have felt as she did about the lighting, and she kept her face

perfectly straight as she responded, 'Third degrees
are more your sort of territory than mine. But, even
so, I suspect that blinding your victim with lights
probably isn't quite your style. I'm sure you go in
for subtler methods of interrogation.'

'You perceive me as subtle?' Again there was
amusement dancing at the back of his eyes.

'Subtle in the same sense as a Venus fly-trap is
subtle. You like to lull your victims into a false sense
of security, then snap your jaws shut on them when
they least expect it.' She smiled a cool smile. 'It
wasn't intended as a compliment.'

'That was to be expected.' Craig smiled at her
irritatingly. 'Compliments, I've noticed, are not
your strong point.'

'Not where you're concerned. You're right about
that. I confess I'd be hard-pressed to find anything
about you to compliment.'

He took a mouthful of his drink. 'Don't let it
bother you. I'm not one of those people who feed
on compliments. I find I can function perfectly well
without them.'

'No doubt you can. With an ego as big as yours,
I'm sure it's quite immaterial to you to win the ap-
proval of others.'

'Quite immaterial.' Still he was smiling, leaning
back against the cushions of the sofa, observing
her with that familiar, arrogant glint in his eye.

And it struck Fiona as she watched him that the
real truth was that he was a man whom it would
be extraordinarily easy to compliment. He was so
striking-looking, he dressed with flair and elegance
and there was just something about him, that sense

of restless energy beneath the calm, unflappable exterior, that attracted admiration like a magnet. It was hard to be with him, to experience his burning aura, and not feel moved to express, with a word or a look, the positive—and, yes, unequivocally complimentary—feelings that rose up inside one, quite unbidden.

Unless, of course, she reminded herself swiftly, one knew what darkness lay hidden behind that bright exterior, the black soul that lurked behind the smile, as she did.

He was looking back at her unblinkingly, quite untouched by her scrutiny, though she suspected he guessed at the thoughts going through her mind. Then he raised one dark eyebrow. 'You're looking charming this evening. That dress you're wearing really is most flattering.'

'I'm so glad you like it.' She instantly wished she hadn't said it, even though her tone was laced liberally with irony. It somehow implied that she was not quite as immune to compliments as he was.

'The colour, above all, is tailor-made for you. It exactly matches the colour of your eyes.'

He was trying to annoy her. She could sense it quite sharply. Poking fun at what he perceived to be her vulnerable female ego.

She grimaced pointedly. 'My, how gallant we are this evening. But, as I pointed out to you just the other day, compliments, when they come from you, somehow lose their sparkle. Try as you might, the insincerity shines through.'

Craig raised one dark eyebrow. 'Insincerity?' he queried. 'I can assure you I don't waste my time with insincere compliments.' Then he smiled at her wickedly. 'You're the one who's insincere. I can remember a time, even if you prefer to forget it, when my compliments could bring tears of pleasure to your eyes.'

Fiona did not have to wonder what he was referring to. He was referring to that day, the day of her confirmation, when she and Craig and Hamish and their parents had set out for the church all together, she all dressed up in her pretty white dress.

'You look wonderful,' he'd told her. 'Like a fairy princess.' And the tears had indeed risen up in her eyes. But then, in the doorway of the church, Hamish, his little mouthpiece, had put her right.

'I probably shouldn't tell you this, but Craig's been killing himself laughing. He thinks you look like a trussed chicken in that outfit!'

And, sure enough, as she'd glanced across at Craig and heard Hamish murmur to him, 'I told her,' she'd seen the look of open amusement in his eyes. And in that instant her whole day had been ruined.

She looked back at him now, feeling the wound fresh inside her. How could he be so deliberately callous as to remind her of that day?

Now such a hurt would simply slide off her. The anger that suddenly swarmed inside her was not for herself, for the woman she had become; rather it was for the pain and the humiliation he had deliberately inflicted on a thirteen-year-old girl.

'You know something . . .?' She paused and narrowed her eyes at him. 'Sometimes I wonder how you have the nerve to look me in the face.' Her expression hardened. 'I suppose it all comes back to the fact that you really don't give a damn about anyone but yourself.'

He had been about to answer. He was leaning towards her, an oddly intent frown on his face. But their hostess chose that moment to come sweeping into the room, buoyed up on a heady cloud of French scent.

'How lovely to see you, Fiona, darling!'

As Fiona rose politely to her feet to greet her, they exchanged make-believe kisses against each other's cheeks. 'I do hope you're hungry?' Doreen glanced across at Craig now, eyelashes fluttering, openly coquettish. Then she was ushering the pair of them towards the dining-room. 'Come, let's get started, before the soufflé spoils!'

At least there was one thing to be said for the evening: Doreen was an excellent cook. And, what was more, she had gone to a great deal of trouble. The dinner she served was perfectly exquisite.

Fiona told her as much as she laid down her dessert spoon after her second delicious helping of chocolate kirsch mousse.

'That was a wonderful meal. I enjoyed every mouthful. You've really done your guests proud, as usual.'

As Doreen smiled, pleased, Fiona almost felt empathy for the woman seated across the table from her. But then, immediately, the misplaced emotion vanished, as Doreen responded, her smile never wavering, 'I think it's important for a woman to be a good cook, to look after her own house, to be a good home-maker.' She touched the stiffly lacquered hair at her temples, sliding a quick glance across at Craig as she continued, 'That's a woman's natural role, as I see it. Women were never meant to do high-powered jobs, to sit in boardrooms and run businesses as men do. It's OK, maybe, for a short while, until they get married, but it's silly for them to think in terms of a long-term career.'

It was not the first such comment that had been made that evening. In fact, there had been so many along these lines that Fiona had rapidly come to the conclusion that the purpose of this cosy little get-together had been to subject her to a bit of brainwashing.

She straightened in her seat, aware that Craig was watching her with an amused expression on his face. 'Surely that depends on the individual woman?' She smiled politely as she said it. She had no desire to get into a fight.

'You mean some women are suited to a career and some aren't, or that some women simply don't have the ability?' Craig glanced from Doreen to Fiona as he said it, deliberately stirring up the antipathy between them.

'I mean both these things.' Fiona kept her gaze steady, in spite of the irritation that was growing inside her. 'Some women have no desire for a career, and that's their choice. I have no problem at all with that. Also, some women, even these days, have insufficient qualifications, and that naturally limits how far they can hope to go. But there are other women who have both the inclination and the ability to carve out serious careers for themselves. And I'm all in favour of them doing just that.'

'But it doesn't work in the long run.' Doreen was insistent. 'Women just aren't psychologically built to cope with the strains and stresses of a career. Sooner or later, they crack. They start making mistakes. They become more of a burden than an asset to their employer. And, really, all they're doing in the end is creating problems for everyone concerned.'

It was the most blatant and direct attack on her yet. Fiona felt the blood surge angrily through her. She looked straight at Doreen. 'Would you by any chance be talking about me? Am I the "they" you keep referring to?' Her tone was clipped, barely civil. 'If so, why don't you just come out and say it?'

'Now I've upset you.' Doreen had the nerve to screw her face into a mask of concern and reach across the table towards her. 'I'm worried about you, that's all,' she said soothingly, as Fiona instantly snatched her hand away. 'Hamish and Craig said you weren't coping. I was just trying in my clumsy old way to give you a bit of friendly advice.'

'That was very kind of you.' Fiona rose to her feet awkwardly and cast a quick glance round the table. 'I won't stay for coffee. I'd like to get home now.' As she stepped away from the table, she smiled a self-mocking smile. 'When you're as incompetent and ill-suited to your job as I am, you need all the rest you can get to help get you through the day.'

Doreen protested, full of humble apologies. 'Don't take on so... It was only you I was thinking of...' But no one seriously tried to stop her as Fiona

strode on rubber legs out into the hallway, knowing
that if she stayed a moment longer she would lose
control of her bubbling anger and might end up
saying something she would later regret. And she
was, after all, a guest in this house.

Hamish materialised from nowhere with her coat,
then stiffly she was bidding goodnight to her hosts,
hurrying out through the front door and heading
for her car.

She heard the front door close as she pulled the
driver's door open and inwardly sighed a sigh of
relief. In a way it would have pleased her to see
them standing there in the cold, politely waving
goodbye, while she drove off down the drive,
pointedly ignoring them. But it pleased her more
that they had gone inside. The very sight of them
infuriated her. She could not bear to look at them.

Fiona shivered as she climbed into the frozen interior of the car and pushed the key into the ignition. All she wanted now was to get safely home,
close the front door behind her and go straight to
bed. Then sleep. She would think about all this in
the morning!

She turned the key in the ignition. Nothing happened. She turned it again and swore softly in the
silence. 'Please start,' she begged, holding her
breath before her third try. 'This would not be a
good moment to let me down.'

But again, as she turned the key, the engine remained silent. There was not even the tiniest
shudder of life.

Fiona leaned back against the seat, squeezing her
eyes shut, as tears of sheer unendurable frustration

threatened to spill. Was she really going to be forced, with her tail between her legs, to go back to the house and ask to use the phone so that she could call for a taxi?

I'd rather walk home! she thought on a surge of bloody-mindedness.

But then suddenly she heard fingers tapping on the side-window, and a voice, slightly muffled through the pane of glass, enquiring, 'Can I be of any assistance?'

CHAPTER SEVEN

IT WAS Craig. Who else? Fiona thought with dull annoyance. Trust him to turn up where he was least wanted. She kept her eyes averted. No doubt he was thoroughly enjoying every second of this further humiliation.

He tapped once more against the window. 'What's up? Won't it start?' Then, to her annoyance, he was pulling open the driver's door. 'Move over. Let me have a go,' he told her.

Fiona sat where she was and glared at him angrily. 'I'll do no such thing. It won't start and that's the end of it. Why on earth should you presume to imagine that it might obligingly start for you?'

He smiled that smile he had the habit of smiling whenever she tried to put him in his place. That smile that irritated her beyond endurance.

'Don't be so damned cussed.' He was leaning against the doorframe, bending towards her, his head inches from her own. 'Just move over and let me have a go, will you? Sometimes another hand on the throttle actually can have a miraculous effect.'

'Especially, no doubt, if the hand happens to be yours.' She was being silly, but she couldn't help it. It was unbearable the way he kept trying to take control.

'Move over, Fiona.' He nudged her gently. 'Or would you rather spend the rest of the night bickering out here in the freezing cold?'

'We don't have to bicker. Why don't you just go back indoors and leave me to deal with this?' She threw him a harsh look. 'I don't need your help.'

'Of course you don't.' But he still hadn't budged a centimetre. And it was the way he continued to stand there, blocking her exit, dark head bent towards her, his eyes fixed on her face, that finally prompted her to surrender.

His nearness seemed to press on her, making her claustrophobic, causing her heart to beat faster in her breast. Unable to bear it a single second longer, Fiona scowled and crossed reluctantly over to the passenger seat, folding her arms across her chest.

'Good girl.' He had slid into the seat beside her, pulling the door shut as he came. Then he was reaching for the starter-key. 'Right,' he murmured. 'Let's see what we can do.'

There was an endless moment of waiting as he twisted the key.

Fiona held her breath.

Nothing happened.

A slow, malicious smile spread over her face. And, as he waited for a moment before having a second try, Fiona was praying with every fibre of her being that his second attempt would prove an equal failure. It was totally illogical, but it was suddenly more important to her that Craig should be thwarted than that she should have the use of her car.

The gods were listening. Her prayers were answered. The engine remained as dead as a dodo.

'Looks like we've had it. It's not going to start. We'd better find another way of getting you home.'

Fiona turned to look at him, unable to hide her pleasure. 'No miracles, after all? How disappointing. So you're not superhuman?'

'Did you think I was? How very flattering.' He caught the gibe neatly and bounced it back at her. 'But you really must learn not to go by appearances.'

Fiona guffawed sarcastically. 'You really love yourself, don't you? Craig Campbell and Craig Campbell, the love-affair of the century!'

He smiled. 'So, after all, we do have something in common.' As she frowned, he elaborated, 'I was referring to a love of self. Don't worry, it's not likely to cross my mind that you share my supposed great love of me. That is something that over the years you've made abundantly clear.'

'Do you blame me?' Fiona shot back at him. There had been something in his tone that had sounded almost like an accusation. She widened her eyes at him. Surely even he couldn't be so totally lacking in self-awareness that he didn't know the reason for her odium?

By way of an answer he narrowed his eyes at her. 'Why——?' he began. Then he stopped himself short. 'Some other time. I'm freezing to death. Let's get back indoors and find a way to get you home.'

As he reached for the door-handle, Fiona remained where she was, staring stubbornly through the windscreen. 'I'm not going back in there. I'm staying right here.' She turned quickly to look at him. 'Perhaps you would do me a favour? Phone for a taxi and I'll wait for it out here.'

'Don't be an idiot. It's about ten below zero. Just swallow your pride and come in for a few minutes.'

Fiona turned sharply away again. 'No, I won't be doing that. I'm sick of swallowing my pride for the Campbells. And if you don't want to phone for a taxi, just tell me. I'll simply walk to the nearest phone-box and phone for one myself.'

'You'll do no such thing. The nearest phone-box is miles away.' He sighed. 'What an infuriatingly stubborn girl you are. Don't you ever do anything anybody wants you to do?'

When she did not answer, he pushed open the door. 'OK, stay there. Freeze to death for all I care. I'll sort something out as quickly as I can.'

As he jumped out of the car and headed back to the house, Fiona sat very still and stared through the windscreen at the bushes all covered with freshly fallen snow. What was that question he had been about to ask her? she found herself wondering, as she huddled down in her seat, pulling the collar of her coat around her ears and plunging her hands deep into her pockets.

Why what? In spite of herself, she was curious. For, somehow, she'd had the feeling that, whatever the question was, it was one that was destined to take her by surprise.

She shrugged and pushed her curiosity from her. More than likely she was destined never to hear the question. He would probably forget he had ever meant to ask it, and she had not the slightest intention of jogging his memory.

Craig was back in what seemed like a couple of minutes.

He tapped on the window and dangled a set of keys. 'I'm borrowing Hamish's car. It's in the garage. Just stay there for a minute till I go round and get it.'

Then he was sprinting across the snow to the other side of the house where the double garage was situated, turning up the collar of the sheepskin jacket that he'd sensibly donned while he was back in the house.

Fiona watched him with oddly mixed feelings. In a way she was grateful that he was taking the trouble to see that she got safely home. She had not really relished in the slightest the prospect of having to trudge to the nearest phone-box. As he had said, it was a couple of miles away.

But at the same time it made her distinctly uneasy to be on the receiving end of his charity. After this, she'd feel indebted to him. Indebted and grateful. And these were not feelings that in the context of Craig Campbell sat either easily or comfortably within her.

Still, it was a bit late now to be having reservations. She could see the nose of Hamish's white Rover appearing round the corner.

She gathered up her bag and stepped out on to the snow as Craig came alongside her, pushing the passenger door open. 'Hop in,' he commanded. Then, as the door slammed shut behind her, they were heading down the wide curved driveway.

Already the car's heater was blasting out warmth, and, as Fiona sank gratefully against the leather seat, she suddenly realised just how cold she had been. She also realised something else.

She reached out her hand to Craig. 'Stop!' she commanded. 'I've left my keys in the ignition!'

'No, you haven't. They're in my pocket.' Craig turned to glance across at her, that familiar, amused smile touching his lips. 'It's just as well one of us knows what he's doing.'

'Then give them to me, please.' Fiona held out her hand to him, pointedly ignoring this little dig.

To her annoyance, he shook his head. 'I'll need them tomorrow morning when I try to get the damned thing started. Unless, of course...' he hesitated meaningfully '...you'd prefer to come over and do that yourself?'

He knew she wouldn't. It was the last thing she'd fancy, an additional visit to Hamish and Doreen's when this one had just proved so catastrophic.

And, yet again, she was torn. Her debt to him was growing. Damn that stupid car! she muttered inwardly. Why did it have to choose tonight of all nights to go and let her down?

It was about a twenty-minute drive back to Bonnie Braes under normal road conditions. But Craig, to Fiona's relief, took the journey slowly, negotiating the icy roads with careful skill, the speedometer scarcely flickering over thirty miles an hour, so that it was nearer forty minutes later that they drew up outside the house.

'Sorry that took so long.' He turned to smile at her. 'I know how anxious you are to get off to bed.'

He was referring to her little outburst back at Hamish and Doreen's, and the unexpected memory of what had prompted it, just for an instant, seemed to catch her by the throat.

Fiona took a deep breath, trying to squash the anger that all of a sudden she could feel rising up inside her. Then with a forced smile she neatly side-stepped the issue and said the first thing that came into her head.

'In these conditions it's better to drive safely and arrive...though I know there aren't many men who think like that.'

'You think we're all speed-fiends?' He was smiling at her, yet seeming to watch her closely through narrowed dark eyes. 'I suppose some of us are. Those with something to prove.'

It was the sort of impossibly arrogant statement that Craig was all too prone to making. I have nothing to prove, was what he was saying. I am totally above all that.

Yet behind the arrogance there was truth in the statement, a truth Fiona reluctantly recognised. She found herself nodding. 'A lot of men seem to think it's terribly macho to scare the living daylights out of their female passengers.'

There was a momentary pause. The dark eyes surveyed her. Then he observed, almost as though he was talking to himself, 'This boyfriend of yours, the one you don't like to talk about, does he suffer from this particular vice?'

She looked at him. 'He did.'

'Did? In the past tense? Does that mean that he finally grew out of it?'

'No. It means that I finally grew out of him.'

Craig laughed. 'I see. It's the boyfriend who's in the past tense.' He continued to look at her. 'And has there been a replacement?'

There had not, but that was none of his business. Let him wonder. Besides, she'd already been far too forthcoming.

Fiona looked straight at him. 'Why are you so curious?'

Craig shrugged. 'What's wrong? It's natural curiosity. One tends to wonder these things about the people one knows.'

'I don't wonder them about you.'

'Don't you?' His eyes narrowed. 'If I may say so, that indicates a remarkably restrained character. Don't you wonder them about anyone, or only about me?'

Fiona ignored that. She had no intention of widening the discussion into an examination of her character.

As though he had never spoken, she added, 'And if I did wonder, I'd have more manners than to start asking questions. I'd show a little respect for your privacy.'

He laughed at the rebuke. 'How very commendable, but, alas, I don't have your refined good manners. Nor your supreme sensitivity,' he added, teasing. 'If you wanted to ask questions, I wouldn't mind in the slightest.'

'But I don't want to ask questions. So, if that was an invitation, I'm afraid, with regret, I must decline it.'

His smile simply seemed to quicken at her sarcasm. 'What a dreadful pity. It might have been rather amusing for the two of us to exchange a couple of confidences.'

There was something about the tenor of the conversation that had caused Fiona's stomach to tighten inexplicably. She felt threatened somehow by his light-hearted banter. The unexpectedness of it, the unfamiliarity of it, made her tense and suddenly wary.

The way he was looking at her, the way he was smiling, could almost pass for a flirtation. And there was only one reason in the world why Craig should play such an unlikely game with her. He was trying to persuade her to lower her defences before striking some deadly underhand blow.

She began to edge away from him, reaching for the door-handle. 'Thank you very much for bringing me home. But, as you said, I'm rather anxious now to get off to bed.'

'Fiona...' As he said it, his expression had subtly altered. There was a strange dark look at the back of his eyes that now shadowed the easy light-heartedness of before.

Here it comes, she thought, as she fumbled with the door-handle, suddenly desperate to escape. For all at once the prospect of the blow she could see coming filled her with an unnatural dread. She could not cope with it now. The smallest hurt would hurt too much.

But, before she could escape, he had reached out and caught her arm. 'Fiona, wait... I have something to say to you.'

It was crazy, but a sudden blind panic tore through her. It took all her will-power to bite back a scream. Controlling herself carefully, she turned round to face him. 'Can't it wait? I'm really rather tired.'

'It won't take a minute.' His fingers still gripped her arm. The expression in his eyes was guarded, unreadable. Then he took a deep breath. 'This evening,' he began, 'Doreen made a remark that might have given you the impression that I'd been discussing you with her...'

He paused, but didn't bother to elaborate. The expression on her face told him she remembered exactly what it was that Doreen had said. *Hamish and Craig said you weren't coping.*

As the words wound through her head, snakelike, full of venom, the fingers around her arm seemed to tighten their grip. 'I just want you to know that what she said isn't so. I never have, and never would, discuss you with Doreen.'

Fiona stared at him, her mind thrown into tiny fragments. Was that it? Just this harmless disavowal? Where was the knife she had expected him to plunge between her ribs?

She frowned at him. 'Is that all? Is that all you wanted to say to me?'

He nodded. 'Yes. Plus the fact, for what it's worth, that neither do I go along with her outdated philosophy that a woman's natural place is in the home.' He smiled. 'But the main thing I wanted to assure you is that I most definitely have not been discussing you with her.' He raised one dark eyebrow. 'I hope you believe me?'

Oddly enough, she had at the moment of telling. Now she felt impatient with her own gullibility.

She slanted him a look. 'I'm really not interested in what goes on between you and Doreen. It doesn't matter a damn to me whether it's true or not.'

'Well, it mattered to me to tell you.' Again his fingers tightened. 'And you ought to believe me. It's the truth, Fiona. I don't discuss matters of business with my brother's wife.'

Matters of business. For some reason, the phrase wounded her. She wanted to turn away, annoyed at her reaction, but the eyes that held hers were like a magnet, drawing her down into their dark, smoky depths.

She felt her resistance to him begin to waver. Perhaps, after all, it *was* safe to believe him. Yet why, she wondered, through the confusion in her brain, should that suddenly matter to her so much?

Then, to her own mild astonishment, she heard herself saying, 'There was something else you were going to say to me...some question you were on the point of asking me back there at your brother's house...'

Craig frowned for just an instant. Then he smiled slowly. 'You mean while we were sitting in your car?'

Fiona nodded. 'Yes. What was it?'

'What was it?' His dark eyes watched her intently. 'If you want to know that, you'll have to invite me in for coffee. It's not the sort of question that can be answered in a couple of minutes.'

Again that sensation of being threatened swam in on her, shark-like, making her heart thud. She was aware that she had allowed herself to be swallowed by those dark eyes, that her body had relaxed into his warm grip on her arm.

She pulled herself up sharply. 'In that case, let's forget it. I'm really not all that interested, anyway.'

'What's the matter; does the thought of inviting me in for coffee alarm you, my dear Fiona? I'm not a rapist. You'd be quite safe, I promise you. And besides . . . forgive me if I contradict you . . . I have the feeling that you really are rather interested.'

'Then your feelings mislead you.' She tried to pull her arm free. The dull thud of her heart had quickened in tempo. The blood seemed to be thundering like an avalanche in her ears. 'And don't believe for a moment that I feel in any way alarmed at the thought of inviting you into my home. I simply find the idea distasteful.'

It wasn't true and he knew it. The thought petrified her for some reason. And his mocking awareness of the illogical panic he had stirred in her was clearly written in his eyes.

'In that case, let's forget it.' There was an amused note in his voice as he let go of her arm and sat back in his seat. He smiled. 'Would you like me to accompany you to your front door?'

'That won't be necessary. Iris will be waiting up for me, and as you can see she's switched on all the outside lights.' That first part wasn't true. As regular as clockwork, Iris was tucked up in bed by ten. But for some reason Fiona was suddenly desperate to escape him. She forced a smile. 'Thanks all the same, but I think I can manage unaccompanied.'

'I'll say goodnight, then.' He turned to look at her.

And then he did something that made her heart fly to her throat.

Still with that amused smile lighting his dark eyes, he leaned towards her and reached out one hand. As his hand brushed her arm, his face inches from her own, suddenly Fiona could no longer control the raging panic that consumed her. She raised one arm quickly as though to defend herself and with her free hand reached out to stop him, punching him in the shoulder.

'Leave me alone! What do you think you're doing?'

Her blow to his shoulder glanced harmlessly off him, scarcely even slowing down his progress as he calmly completed what he had been doing—opening the passenger door for her.

'I thought,' he observed equably, as the door swung open, 'I ought to give you a gentlemanly hand. You seemed to be having a little trouble finding the handle.'

What a fool she felt! What an unspeakable idiot! And he proceeded to make her feel even more ridiculous as he smiled and observed, 'You really ought to try to curb that tendency of yours to get physical. One of these days you might just find yourself up against someone with similar tendencies.'

Fiona was out of the car before he could say more. 'Goodnight,' she muttered in the general direction of the car. 'And thanks for giving me a lift.'

Then she was hurrying swiftly across the soft snow, eyes fixed straight ahead, legs quivering like jellies, her heart beating frantically, like a trapped bird, inside her, eyes blind, her progress guided by habit.

She was aware of him waiting till she was safely inside before he turned the car round and headed back to the main road. But she did not turn to look at him, nor to wave from the doorway, but closed the door behind her without even a glance.

Then, eyes shut tight, she leaned her back against the door, dropped her bag to the floor and stood for several minutes, breathing rhythmically, deeply and slowly, until at last the storm in her had passed.

But what had caused the craziness? she wondered later, lying in her bed, unable to sleep. What had triggered off that torrent of emotion that had caused her to make such a spectacular fool of herself?

For she really had believed that Craig had been about to kiss her, when nothing, surely, had been further from his mind. And that semi-flirtatious exchange earlier on had caused her not only, she realised now, to feel threatened by the suspicion that he was out to disarm her all the more effectively to stick a knife between her ribs, but also, far more significantly, it had caused her to feel threatened by him as a man.

How odd. How alarming. How inexplicable. She tossed and turned beneath the bedclothes. Craig certainly did not regard her as a woman—in the sense of being a warm, sensitive, sexual being. All she was and had ever been to him was a nuisance to be trodden underfoot.

And her feelings about him were correspond-
ingly asexual. He was simply a cruel bully who had
to be resisted. He was the bane of her life whom
she would long ago have left behind her, had it not
been for their unfortunate professional association. And she had never thought of him as anything other than that.

So why had she almost literally gone to pieces
when he had held her and spoken to her as he had,
then leaned towards her as though to kiss her? For
the fear in her had been blatantly sexual. Nothing
to do with anything else.

And why, above all, had she not reacted as she
would have done with any other man whose sexual
advances she did not wish to encourage? As she
had, for example, with Hamish earlier? Why hadn't
she just cut him with a cold glance and warned him
to back off and not play games with her?

It's because of this sword he's holding over my
head, this threat to push me out of the company.
I feel beleaguered, confused, pushed into a corner.
No wonder I was unable to react straightforwardly!

This explanation soothed her. It was solid. It
made sense. She hugged it to her, along with her
pillow, steadfastly ignoring that corner of her mind
that still nagged and hovered around a very different truth, until at last, too exhausted to think
any more, she drifted off into merciful sleep.

CHAPTER EIGHT

THE next day, thank heavens, was Friday.

Fiona was starting to feel as though her brain was overheating. There were too many pressures bearing down on her now. The threat of losing her job. The business with Hamish. And now this new anxiety that was assailing her—the fear of having to face Craig again that was far stronger than the other two put together.

It was a fear that literally filled her mind, and she simply could not understand it.

Fortunately, on that final day of the working week, not only did she not come face to face with Craig, but she also saw him only once, hurrying towards his office, head bent, so that she was spared even the discomfort of having to greet him.

She was less fortunate in her efforts to avoid his brother. Twice she came back from visits to other departments to find Hamish hovering outside her office door.

He eyed her sleazily as she swept briskly past him and demanded, 'Is there anything I can do for you?'

It was an unfortunate choice of words, as she realised instantly. He stepped towards her as she stood facing him by her desk. 'You know what you can do for me, Fiona. Let's not beat about the bush.' He winked. 'How about a little drink after work? And then…' he winked again '…after that, who knows?'

'The answer's no.' She regarded him squarely, controlling her anger, keeping her voice low. 'When will you learn to take no for an answer?'

'Perhaps when you've managed to convince me that you mean it. Right now, you're only playing hard to get. Just as well for both of us that I don't give up easily.'

'I do mean it, Hamish. Please don't fool yourself. Just take my word for it and stop wasting your time.'

They were interrupted as one of the phones on her desk began to ring. As she reached to pick it up, he held her eyes and smiled. 'See you later.' It sounded like a threat. And then, with a last sleazy look, he left the room.

Fiona had never been more relieved when she glanced at her watch some time later and discovered it was almost six o'clock. Time to go home. She stretched her arms above her head. Time for the weekend. She smiled with relief. Time to forget all her problems for a while.

Back home she showered and changed and chatted with Iris for a while before sitting down to a delicious dinner of roast chicken and treacle pudding.

But, for once, she was unable to do Iris's cooking full justice. As she carried her plates back to the kitchen, Iris frowned. 'What's the matter? Aren't you feeling well, Miss MacGregor? You've barely tasted any of it.'

'I know. I'm sorry. Save it for tomorrow. For some reason I just don't feel hungry this evening. Maybe I'm over-tired.' She gave Iris a small hug. 'I'm sorry. After all the trouble you've gone to.'

'What does that matter?' Iris clucked impatiently. 'The only thing that matters is your health.' She frowned again. 'You've been looking a bit peaky lately. You work too hard. You should give yourself a rest.'

Fiona smiled. 'I plan to. I'm going to have a lazy weekend. So don't worry. I'll be as fit as a fiddle again by Monday.'

But, in spite of her promise to have a lazy weekend, that evening she simply could not relax. She tried to settle in front of the TV, but every five minutes she would be jumping to her feet to make herself some coffee, pour herself a drink, or rifle through the magazines on the table.

She felt jumpy, a bag of nerves. I won't sleep, she thought irritably. Her brain was whirring round and round.

There was nothing else for it. Just after nine o'clock she switched off the TV and tossed the magazines on the floor. Perhaps if she took herself out for a jog, a brisk half-hour in the clean evening air, that would help to settle her mental fidgeting.

She rushed upstairs and changed into her blue tracksuit, with a warm polo-neck sweater underneath for extra warmth, pushed her feet in their woolly socks into her trainers and secured her blonde hair beneath a wide blue headband.

Back downstairs she tapped on Iris's door. 'I'm just going out jogging for half an hour. I think I need a bit of fresh air.'

It was a beautiful night, clear and crisp and clean, with a huge pale moon floating high in the sky and clusters of stars twinkling like jewels between the clouds.

The snow had stopped falling, but it lay all round, wreathing the landscape in a deep, ethereal silence, blurring the boundaries between hedgerows and gardens, even causing the land and the heavens to appear as one.

She took her usual route along the well-lit pavements that more or less circled Bonnie Braes. It was about three miles in all if she took the detour past Jock's Dairy.

That was the route she was intending to take now, as she set off down the road at a steady rhythm, pacing herself carefully, not taking the run too fast, loving the surge of energy that drove through her, the warmth of her blood as it tingled through her veins.

And almost instantly she began to feel better as the knots of tension inside her slackened. She could feel her brain clearing as she breathed in deeply. A stab of exhilaration and release went through her. Why hadn't she thought of doing this earlier?

It was as she turned the corner, heading for the dairy, that she heard a swish of tyres behind her. She didn't turn round. In fact, she thought nothing of it. This, after all, was a residential neighbourhood. You expected to encounter the occasional car.

But then she was aware of the vehicle slowing and drawing into the kerb alongside her. With a stab of anxiety she whirled round sharply and in that instant her anxiety turned to anger.

'What the hell do you think you're playing at?' As she recognised in a flash Hamish's familiar white Rover she turned on it furiously and thumped the bonnet. And suddenly she was remembering all too clearly his earlier threat: 'I'll see you later.'

'I'm getting sick of this!' she screamed. 'I'm going to report you! I'll have you locked up if you don't leave me alone!'

But an instant later she stopped in her tracks as the driver's window slid down and she realised her mistake.

Craig leaned out and frowned at her. 'What the devil's got into you? Have you taken leave of your senses?'

She'd made an idiot of herself again, Fiona thought with sharp annoyance. 'I thought you were someone else,' she answered stonily. 'And anyway you frightened me, creeping up on me like that.'

'I didn't mean to frighten you and I apologise if I did. I called at the house and Iris told me you were out jogging. I simply meant to surprise you, not to give you a fright.'

Then he smiled at her teasingly. 'Who did you think I was? Did you think I was that poor, heart-broken ex-boyfriend of yours come to carry you away?'

No, I thought you were your lecherous damned brother! Fiona was tempted for a moment to tell him the truth. She looked into his smiling, arrogant face. How would he react, she wondered, if she did?

But she knew how he would react. He would not believe her. He would refuse to hear a bad word spoken against Hamish.

So she saved herself the aggro of a pointless discussion. 'No,' she answered simply, then demanded, frowning, 'What the devil do you want with me anyway?'

'A word.' He smiled and leaned towards the car door. 'Come on. Jump in. I'll give you a lift home.'

'A word?' Fiona glared at him. 'Why don't you just leave me alone? I don't happen to want a word with you!' She turned away angrily and resumed her jogging. 'And I can get home under my own steam, thank you all the same!'

The car was moving forward, slowly, to keep level with her. 'In that case, I'll wait for you at the house.'

The window slid closed again. He probably didn't hear her angry response, 'Please don't bother!'

Fiona watched the car disappear down the road, her earlier tranquillity now totally shattered. She felt twice as tense as she had before her jog, her limbs as tight as drawn elastic, the drumming in her brain an almost audible din.

Why had he come here? What the devil did he want with her? Mentally, she kissed goodbye to her peaceful weekend.

Fiona had hoped that by some miracle the white Rover wouldn't be waiting when she got back to Bonnie Braes, that he might have changed his mind and gone straight home, deciding to leave her in peace for once. But there it was, parked in the driveway, with a trail of fresh footprints leading through the snow from the car right up to the red front door. No doubt he was sitting ensconced by the fireside with a glass of her best twelve-year-old whisky in his hand.

He was, and he looked so easy and comfortable, dressed in grey trousers and a burgundy cashmere sweater, that one might easily have believed he had every right to be there.

He smiled as she poked her head into the sitting-room. 'Iris let me in. I hope you don't mind. And she insisted on pouring me a glass of Glenmorangie.'

Fiona looked right through him. 'I'm going upstairs for a shower. If you get bored waiting, feel free to leave any time.'

'Oh, I won't get bored.' He stretched his legs out in front of him and settled himself more comfortably in his chair. 'Just you run along and take as long as you please. I promise I'll still be here waiting for you.'

Fiona retreated, grimacing. Was that a promise or a threat? It had sounded rather like the latter!

In fact, though she was sorely tempted to linger and put off the evil moment of confrontation as long as possible, Fiona showered quickly, pulled on a loose blue kaftan and was downstairs again in less than fifteen minutes.

'That was quick.' Craig raised an amused dark eyebrow. 'What's up? Couldn't you bear to stay away?'

Fiona crossed to the bar and poured a Cinzano and soda, deliberately turning her back as she did so. 'What a quaint idea. But the truth is less romantic. I simply figured that the sooner I got down here again the sooner you could tell me what it is you've come for...' she paused and turned to slide a mocking glance at him '...and the sooner you could be on your way again.'

'How very inhospitable.'

Fiona smiled. 'Yes, isn't it? Isn't it strange how you effect me that way?'

'Most strange. It's not the way I affect most women. Most women, I find, simply can't have enough of me.'

'They're welcome to all of you, as far as I'm concerned.' She smiled at her own witticism as she crossed the deep wine carpet and seated herself in one of the armchairs opposite him. 'That way I'd be spared these unexpected little visits.' She crossed her knees beneath the blue cotton kaftan and took a small sip of her Cinzano and soda. 'Which brings me straight to the point... What are you doing here?'

'I've come to see you.'

'I gathered that. But why?'

'Maybe I just felt like half an hour of your charming company.'

'And pigs might fly.' Fiona pulled a wry face at him. 'What piece of bad news have you come to lay before me this time?'

He regarded her for a moment, his dark eyes narrowing. Then he smiled and let his gaze sweep round the room. 'I'd forgotten how lovely this house is. It's years since I've been in it. And this, I have to say, is a charming room.'

'I'm glad you think so.' Her tone was sarcastic.

'But it is, don't you think, a little large for one?'

Something jolted inside her, a kind of mingled fear and panic. She swallowed it down. 'There are two of us,' she reminded him tartly. 'You're forgetting that Iris lives here, too.'

'Ah, yes; Iris.' He continued to look at her, a dark, shuttered look about his eyes. 'But, as I keep telling you, surely Iris is a rather unnecessary extravagance now that you're on your own?'

Anger surged within her. It was none of his damned business why she chose to keep Iris on. She said, 'I suppose, down in London, you do all your own cooking and cleaning? I suppose you wouldn't dream of having domestic help?'

He smiled. 'I'm afraid I do. But that's a little different.'

'Why? Because you're a man, or because you're Craig Campbell? Are there different rules for you?'

He shrugged. 'I need someone to look after the house when I'm away, which I am quite a lot. But she doesn't live in. I don't allow myself that luxury.' He paused and looked at her. 'Why do you?'

'Because I'm lazy and spoiled and utterly useless around the house, as well as being totally incompetent at my job!' Her fingers tightened around her glass as she shot the words at him. Let him hear what he wanted to hear. He wouldn't listen to the truth! Her eyes glinted across at him, full of accusation. 'I'm rather surprised you need to have it spelled out.'

'I just like to get things clear. From the horse's mouth.' He gazed for a moment into her stiff, angry face. 'Who did you think I was when I surprised you out jogging? Who is this poor individual who inspires such fierce anger in you?'

'Someone.'

'Which someone? Not your old boyfriend?'

'I already told you it wasn't my old boyfriend.'

'You might have been misleading me. You're so reluctant to talk about him.'

'Why should I need to talk about him? There's nothing to talk about.'

'Nothing?'

'Nothing.' She looked back at him unblinkingly. 'He was one of those men who was all façade, with absolutely nothing underneath.' She'd been about to add, 'Like you', but had stopped herself, knowing that such an insult would be grossly inaccurate.

Craig was not what he seemed, but he was far from being a cipher. Alan *had* been a cipher, a big, empty nothing.

She smiled. 'Don't worry about him. He was only too relieved when I finally let him go off to find himself a female who was rather more easily impressed than me.'

If it sounded glib, the glibness was intentional. There was no need at all for Craig to know the bitter disappointment she had felt when she'd discovered that Alan was just like the others—an immature boy, simply playing at being a man. She'd already had more than her fill of those.

Craig was smiling that arrogant, irritating smile of his as he regarded her over the rim of his whisky glass. 'So, you consider yourself to be a woman who's not easily impressed? That's interesting.' As he paused, his smile hardened at the corners. 'And I'll bet you don't hesitate to let them know you're not impressed. Poor devils. Sensitivity was never your strong point.'

He had said that once before. Or something very similar. And that other time she had simply let the comment pass. This time she did not.

'And what is that supposed to mean? Or is it just one of your random insults?'

'Not random, no. Quite specific. And it wasn't meant as an insult. Merely an observation.' He smiled a harsh smile. 'For all I know, you take great pride in your insensitivity.'

'I wasn't aware it was a quality I possessed.'

She said 'quality' deliberately, rather than 'fault', in order to demonstrate that she didn't give a damn what insults or criticisms he cared to hurl at her. But the truth was she found the accusation deeply wounding. No one had ever called her insensitive before, and, in a way, it was the worst insult she could think of.

His eyes were cruel. 'In that case, I would suggest that you still have a lot to learn about yourself. Personally, I've known you possessed that particular quality for a very great number of years.'

He had pushed the knife deeper and given it a vicious twist. She was surprised at the ferocity of the pain that tore through her. After all, hadn't she always known how much he hated and despised her? Surely, by now, she ought to be immune?

Perhaps mercifully, at that moment the drawing-room door opened and Iris poked her head inside. 'Will there be anything else, Miss MacGregor? Shall I make you both some coffee? Or maybe Mr Campbell would like a bite to eat?'

If he did, he could go hungry! Fiona thought to herself with venom, as she swivelled round in her chair to address Iris. 'No, we won't be needing you. You go off to bed now. And thanks for looking after Mr Campbell while I was upstairs.'

'Don't mention it. My pleasure. Goodnight to both of you.' Then, with a smile and a nod, Iris disappeared.

Fiona turned back to Craig, her eyes as hard as granite. She could still feel the throb of the hurt he had inflicted, and suddenly, overpoweringly, she wanted rid of him.

'I think you'd better go. I'm really very tired. Perhaps you wouldn't mind just finishing your drink?'

His eyes swept over her. She could not tell what he was thinking. He said, deliberately ignoring her suggestion, 'Aren't you interested to know what brings me here?'

'Not in the slightest.' She could not resist adding, 'There's nothing about you that could possibly interest me.'

He smiled, infuriatingly. 'Yes, you said that before. But that wasn't always so.' He leaned back in his chair. 'I can remember a time when I seemed to interest you rather a lot.'

'Like when?'

'When you were small.'

'I think your memory's playing tricks with you.'

'Not at all. I remember it all very clearly. In the early days, when you used to come to visit our house, you used to follow me around, asking me endless questions, wanting to know all about all the things I was doing.' He smiled. 'There was no sign of lack of interest then.'

Was that true? Something jolted uncomfortably inside her. A memory, half smothered, long forgotten.

'I must have been retarded,' she answered in a clipped tone.

'Not at all. On the contrary, you were a very bright child. Warm and friendly and utterly charming. And then...' He paused and looked at her. 'Then something happened. You changed. You became nasty and spiteful and vindictive.' He frowned at her. 'What on earth happened, Fiona?'

Her heart was beating strangely. Resentfully, she glared at him. 'You mean, why did I stop following you around like a puppy? Why did I stop worshipping you as if you were some kind of god?'

She felt her throat constrict, the words almost choking her, for suddenly she was remembering far more than she cared to. She *had* adored him. She had worshipped him totally. But she had crushed it from her memory. And no wonder. The memory shamed her.

Her violet eyes flashed at him. 'I'll tell you why I changed! I changed because I realised what an idiot I'd been! I realised how blind I'd been, how pathetically impressionable, and that you were no more worthy of my respect and admiration than the dirt beneath my shoes!' She snatched a gasp of breath. 'So, now you have your answer! Now you know why I suddenly became immune to your charm and stopped being so interested in everything you did!'

A silence fell. Profound and endless. One could almost hear the snow outside falling.

Then Craig said simply, 'You're right. Now I know.' His dark eyes on her, he drained his glass quickly. 'I see no reason to detain you any longer.'

Fiona rose to her feet. 'I'll get your coat.'

Then she was leading him out into the hallway, rigid with relief and still-bubbling anger, scarcely able to contain her need to be rid of him. She took his coat from the cloakroom and thrust it at him almost roughly, then waited impatiently by the front door as he took his time about pulling it on.

'Goodnight.' As he headed unhurriedly towards her, she snatched the door open and stood stiffly aside. She was suddenly so tense that she was almost bursting.

But as he was striding past her, suddenly he paused. He looked down into her face. 'You didn't answer my question.'

Fiona felt her jaw clench. Her hand on the door trembled. 'And what question would that be?' she answered angrily.

'Who did you think I was when I surprised you out jogging? I'm curious. Your reaction was quite spectacular.'

Curious, was he? She raised her eyes to look at him, and suddenly her impatience and her anger made her reckless.

'I thought you were your brother.' The words were a catharsis. 'I thought he'd come round to keep his promise.'

'My brother?' She had the pleasure of seeing real surprise on his face. 'And what promise did you think he'd come here to keep?'

'His promise to keep hounding me and making cheap passes at me in an effort to try and get me into bed.' Fiery-eyed, Fiona spilled the whole lot out to him. 'Presumably, he thinks if he keeps it up long enough, I won't be able to stand it and I'll end up quitting my job.'

Craig leaned past her and pushed the door to. 'My brother has been trying to get you into bed?'

The last thing she had imagined was that he would listen. She had fully expected that he would cut her off short. But there he stood before her, waiting for her answer, neither denying what she was saying, nor showing any sign of anger.

She felt her own anger leave her at this opportunity to unburden herself, and a sense almost of gratitude to have a willing ear.

'It's been going on for about three months now. He's been driving me crazy. Catching me off guard at odd moments in the office, sneaking up on me in the car park, trying to lay his filthy hands all over me. No wonder,' she protested, 'I've been making mistakes. No wonder I've been finding it hard to concentrate.'

'And have any of these episodes been what you might call serious? I mean, has he actually sexually assaulted you?'

'Once he came close.' At the memory her heart beat faster. Disgust drove through her. She felt her breath catch. 'Once he really scared me——' She broke off suddenly and forced herself to look into Craig's eyes.

'That was the day I made that mistake about the prices. I was so upset I just couldn't think straight.'

Craig's expression had never altered. The dark eyes were unblinking. 'Was that the little episode in the copying-room? Would that be the particular incident you're referring to?'

She didn't stop to think how he could possibly know that. Fiona nodded her head. 'Yes, that was it.'

'It was after hours, most of the other staff had gone home and the two of you found yourselves in the copying-room together...?'

'It wasn't quite like that. *I* was in the copying-room, and——'

'You mean *my brother* was in the copying-room and you came in behind him...?'

'No, *I* was there first. He came in behind *me*.'

'You closed the door.' She might as well not have spoken. 'And then you proceeded to take off your blouse.'

'I what? It was Hamish who tried to rip it off my back!'

'You were wearing a lacy bra. It was a pink one, I believe.' The dark eyes flayed her. 'That detail is correct?'

Fiona felt the colour rise and ebb in her face. 'I hardly think such details matter——'

'But it was pink, wasn't it?'

'Yes, I believe so.'

'Then, as my brother stood there, horrified, you removed the pink bra and, bare-breasted, proceeded to make certain exceedingly direct sexual advances.'

Fiona could not speak.

Craig smiled. 'My brother tells me you have a perfectly exquisite body. Full, well-shaped breasts. No wonder you thought he'd be tempted. After all, many men might consider it a fair exchange... many men would undoubtedly be sorely tempted to accept the offer to taste its myriad pleasures in exchange for agreeing to turn a blind eye to the owner's total professional incompetence.' His lips thinned. 'My brother, however, was not one of them.'

Fiona found her voice. 'He told you that?'

'Do you deny it?'

She was trembling. 'Every foul word of it.'

'I thought you might. That's why I wasn't going to bother telling you. But you insisted on bringing up the subject, in a crude effort to blacken my brother's name.'

He pulled the door open. 'I'll bid you goodnight now.'

Then, leaving her stranded in the doorway, sick in her soul and numb from head to toe, he turned on his heel and strode out into the night, his footsteps in the snow as silent as her dead heart.

CHAPTER NINE

FIONA lay in bed and simmered that night. It wasn't until almost four in the morning that, finally, she fell asleep. Then, about ten o'clock, she awoke with a start, and in a flash she knew exactly what she must do.

She jumped out of bed and headed for the shower, her brain suddenly clear, in spite of the lack of sleep. She couldn't let Craig get away scot-free with those shameful accusations he had hurled at her last night. She would not stand for it. She had stood for too much already. She would speak to him, at once, and put him right!

After her shower she dressed quickly in a pair of forest-green wool trousers, a matching cashmere sweater and a pair of high tan boots. Then, grabbing her tan shoulder-bag, she hurried downstairs, calling to Iris as she went.

'Iris, I'm going out. I don't know when I'll be back. I'll give you a ring to let you know about dinner.'

'Never mind dinner. What about breakfast?' Iris had appeared in the drawing-room doorway. 'You can't go out on an empty stomach in weather like this.'

But Fiona was already taking her coat from the cloakroom, pulling it on and taking her gloves from the pockets.

'I'll have something to eat later, Iris. Don't worry about me. Just you put your feet up and have a nice lazy day.'

'It's that Craig Campbell, isn't it? It's something to do with him?' Iris scowled with concern as Fiona headed for the front door. 'I knew he was trouble last night as soon as I saw him.'

Fiona paused and smiled at her. 'Don't worry, Iris, really. There's just a small misunderstanding I have to sort out.'

Small! She smiled grimly as she hurried down the steps, heading for her little red car, which Craig had returned to her yesterday. What she had to sort out with Craig was a mountain of misunderstanding, dating right back to the days of her childhood!

For she had decided not only to tackle him about last night, but about all her grievances accumulated over the years. It was time she confronted him with, in all its sordid detail, the catalogue of hurt and humiliation he had inflicted and which, until now, she had only ever hinted at.

The Renault, to her delight, started instantly. Then she was heading down the drive, then taking the east road through the town, driving carefully through the thinly falling snow.

She parked outside the main gates of the old Campbell residence, intending to sneak unseen round to the back of the house, then to the granny house at the foot of the garden. She had no desire to speak to either Hamish or Doreen.

But she had gone barely two steps down the crazy-paved path when the front door opened and

Doreen was standing there. She smiled a false smile. 'Why, Fiona, what a surprise! What brings you here on a Saturday morning?'

Reluctantly, Fiona stepped up to the front door to greet her. 'I've come to see Craig. I didn't mean to bother you.' She smiled and took a step towards the back path. 'I'll just go straight round, if you don't mind.'

'You won't find him there. He's gone off skiing.' Doreen looked pleased to be able to give her this bad news. 'I'm afraid he left a couple of hours ago.'

Fiona's heart sank. 'Where was he going? Did he tell you which slopes he was heading for?'

'Funny...' Doreen leaned insolently against the door-jamb '...you're the second lady visitor he's had this morning. The other one just missed him as well. Our Craig appears to be a very popular fellow.'

'Did he say where he was going?' Fiona repeated her question. Craig's popularity with the ladies was not something that interested her.

Doreen shrugged. 'He said something about Aviemore. He has a friend who has a chalet up there.'

'Thanks.' Fiona had turned and was heading down the path again. It was a good two hours' drive to Aviemore. With luck, she should be there a little after lunchtime.

She was lucky. The roads, for the most part, were clear. The snowploughs had been out earlier that morning. It was just before two when Fiona drove into Aviemore, the once modest little Highland village, nestling among the snow-clad mountains, that had become Scotland's favourite ski resort.

Fiona knew where she was going. To the big mountainside car park that stood next to the main ski-lift station. Most of the resort's skiers passed through there, and that was where she would wait for Craig.

She had parked as near as she could to the station, with a clear view of the skiers coming and going—in laughing groups, skis slung over their shoulders, the loose metal fastenings of their stiff, heavy boots clanking softly as they walked.

And now she was huddled in the front seat of her car, a plaid rug wrapped around her shoulders, stamping her feet against the cold. Let him come soon, she prayed beneath her breath. Please let him come before I freeze to death!

By four o'clock it was starting to grow dark and the steady flow of skiers returning from the slopes was rapidly turning into a flood. But still there was no sign of him, and with the chaos all around her of skiers returning to their cars Fiona was starting to worry that she might have missed him.

She sighed inwardly. If she had, there was nothing for it but to return to her vigil first thing tomorrow morning and try to catch him on the way in.

And then, just as she was about to give up hope, she caught sight of him, striding across the car park, about twenty yards off to her right.

Instantly, Fiona was clambering out of her plaid rug and reaching anxiously for the door-handle. But something made her pause to watch him for a moment, almost to savour his progress across the snow.

He was wearing a plain dark navy ski-suit with a bright red ski-cap covering his dark hair, his goggles pushed up to the top of his head. And he was striding like a big cat across the car park, his skis and sticks balanced over one shoulder, loose-limbed, a light, vibrant spring in his step, the lithe, faintly arrogant gait of a man who was at the peak of physical fitness.

Her stomach squeezed strangely. This was the man she so hated. And for the first time ever it struck her as regrettable that what she knew about him precluded for ever the possibility of her reacting to him as the virile, attractive man he surely was.

What a shame, she thought almost wistfully. What a terrible waste.

She did not allow that thought to linger. She pushed it from her and stepped out on to the snow.

'Craig!' She cupped her hands to her mouth and called to him. 'Craig!' she called again, as he frowned and turned around.

'Fiona. What the——?' He scowled and strode towards her. His eyes were full of questions. 'What the devil are you doing here?'

'I came to speak to you.' She felt oddly vulnerable, standing there huddled in her heavy camel coat. He seemed in his element, a polar cat amid the snow. By contrast, she felt disadvantaged, ill at ease.

Craig glanced past her to her car. 'You drove up here in that?' He smiled an odd smile. 'Whatever's brought you here must be important.'

'It is.' She held his gaze. 'Very important. Can we go back to wherever it is you're staying?'

In answer he frowned at her. 'Has something happened? To Hamish or Doreen or the kids?'

'No, nothing's happened.' The question irked her. Did his first thought always have to be for that wretched brother of his?

'Then what do you want to see me for?' His eyes were still full of questions, but there was none of the hostility she had expected, none of the caustic anger of last night.

Fiona stamped her frozen feet and huddled deeper into her coat. 'Can't we go somewhere warm and discuss this?' she almost pleaded. 'I've been sitting here waiting for you for two and a half hours.'

His frown deepened. A strange look crossed his eyes. 'It really must be important,' he murmured. Then he shrugged. 'OK. That's my car over there.' He pointed to a Land Rover, parked just a few yards behind her. 'I hired it for the weekend,' he explained. Then he hurried on, 'Follow me back down to the village in your car. I'll take it slowly and try not to lose you.'

That final promise was made with a wry smile that had caused Fiona to wonder cynically, as they set off down the winding mountain road, whether what he really intended was the opposite! After all, to be rid of her was what he more habitually aimed for!

But she was still clinging like a limpet to the red tail-lights of the Land Rover when at last it turned into Aviemore's main street, heading towards the other end of the village.

A few minutes later they had turned off the main road to where a cluster of pretty wooden chalets were arranged, and Craig was drawing up in front of one of them.

He climbed out of the Land Rover. 'This is it!' he called to her. Then he was striding through the snow towards the front door, sticking the key in the lock and pushing the door open.

With a smile, he stood aside as she hurried to join him. 'After you,' he invited. 'Be my guest.'

The warmth of the central heating enveloped her like a mantle. Blissfully, Fiona could feel her frozen muscles relax. Her solidified feet began to tingle.

'Make yourself at home. I'm going to have a quick shower.' Craig winked and pointed towards the kitchen. 'And if you're feeling generous, perhaps you wouldn't mind making us both a cup of hot chocolate?'

He had propped his skis and sticks in a corner of the vestibule and was bending down now to pull off his boots, before snatching the goggles and woolly hat from his head. 'If you have a rake around,' he added, hanging up the hat and starting to unzip his navy anorak, 'perhaps you could dig up a piece of cake or some biscuits? I could do with a bite to eat.'

Standing there, dressed only in the tight-fitting ski-pants and the body-hugging roll-neck top, he looked, Fiona thought, totally ravishing. Every inch of him prime, powerful male.

The thought appalled her. She turned away abruptly, averting her eyes and heading for the kitchen. 'Hot chocolate coming up.' Her voice sounded croaky. She was glad he couldn't see that her cheeks had turned crimson.

By the time he reappeared she had regained her composure and was sitting at the coffee-table in the living-room, her coat and boots shed and, laid out before her, a pot of hot chocolate and a plate of thickly sliced Dundee cake.

'Good girl. That looks and smells delicious.'

He had changed into a pair of tobacco cord trousers and a loose-fitting roll-neck camel sweater, yet, as Fiona glanced up at him, for an instant in her mind's eye she saw him again in the muscle-moulding ski-pants and tight top that had so upset her equilibrium earlier.

Shame on you! she chastised herself, reaching for the hot chocolate and, with an unsteady hand, pouring two mugfuls. You're behaving like a panting adolescent!

She pushed a mug towards him, as he seated himself in the armchair opposite her, and observed in a suitably neutral tone, 'This is a lovely little chalet. It belongs to a friend of yours, I believe?'

'That's right.' He took the mug from her and helped himself to cake. 'He's in the States at the moment. He said I could borrow it.'

It was odd, she had assumed that he'd be staying here alone, yet for some reason she felt a strange *frisson* go through her, almost a sense of secret pleasure that they were unlikely to be interrupted.

The reason for that, she quickly assured herself, was that her business here was private. Nothing else.

He was leaning back in his chair, taking a mouthful of his cocoa. 'I often stay here. As you say, it's very comfortable. And it couldn't be more convenient for the skiing.'

That surprised her. 'I didn't know you came here often. I thought that these days you tended to stay south of the border.'

Craig shrugged. 'My work tends to keep me in London, but I come up to Scotland whenever I have some time off.'

I never see you. She almost said it. But of course she never saw him. She had no wish to see him. And, what was more, she had no interest in the private details of his life.

Fiona nodded. 'I see.' She clasped her hands around her cocoa-cup. It was time she got down to what she was here for. The atmosphere was getting just a little too cosy.

She cleared her throat. 'There's something I need to speak to you about.' As she said it, she raised her eyes to his and hated the way her heart skittered inside her.

Nerves, she decided, tucking a strand of hair behind her ear. She was not looking forward to another angry confrontation.

'So I gather.' He bit into his Dundee cake and chewed thoughtfully, watching her, for a moment. 'I'm sure you didn't come all this way just to have a cup of cocoa.'

As he said it, he smiled, which only made her more nervous. Fiona checked herself impatiently.

What was the matter with her? Where was the resolve that she had awakened with this morning? Why wasn't she tearing his eyes out in anger?

She laid down her mug, then sat back in her chair, with an effort of will-power conquering her nervousness. She looked Craig in the eye. 'It's about last night.' She felt pleased with the hard edge to her voice as she continued, 'You made certain accusations about my conduct with your brother. I've come here to tell you that I won't tolerate such a slander. Regardless of what he might have told you, there's not a word of truth in that shameful, disgusting story.'

'Isn't there?'

'No.'

'You're quite sure of that, are you?'

He had not moved. His eyes had never left her. His tone was neutral, devoid of all emotion.

'Of course I'm sure!' Fiona's tone was impatient. 'How could I not be sure about something like that?'

'Quite so.' The dark eyes continued to watch her. Then he sighed and leaned forward to lay down his cocoa-cup, pausing to scrutinise her for just a moment longer. 'If I was wrong, then I apologise.' He sat back in his seat. 'If I was wrong, I should never have said what I did.'

Fiona was momentarily struck dumb. This was the last thing she had expected. An admission of culpability and, even more astonishing, an apology!

Only it wasn't really an admission of culpability, she suddenly realised, no more than it was a proper apology.

She looked into his face, her expression an accusation. 'What do you mean *if* you were wrong?' she demanded. 'What sort of apology is that?'

His eyes seemed to narrow. 'It's the best I can offer. It's up to you. Take it or leave it.'

'Then I'll leave it!' She glared at him furiously across the coffee-table. 'If that's the best you can offer, it doesn't mean a thing!'

'What do you want me to do—get down on my knees and grovel? Do you want me to kiss your feet and beg for your forgiveness?'

'All I want...' she breathed angrily, her hands clenching in her lap '... all I want is for you to have the decency to admit you were wrong and offer a proper apology. I don't really think that's too much to ask!'

'Well, I'm afraid it is.' His eyes had grown steely. 'I said if I was wrong, then I apologise. I can't do any better than that.'

'You could cut the "if".' She ground the words at him. 'Just for once you could admit straight out that you were wrong!'

'And how the hell am I supposed to know if I was wrong?' With an impatient gesture he sprang to his feet, thrusting his fists into the pockets of his trousers. 'I wasn't there! I didn't see what happened between you! I'm prepared to acknowledge that I might have been wrong, that what Hamish told me wasn't accurate. Surely that ought to be enough for you?'

Yes, probably it ought. After all, it was a lot. The thought went through Fiona's head as she continued to scowl up at him. After all, when before,

in all the years she had known him, had she ever
heard him cast doubt on Hamish's testimony? The
answer to that was simple.

Never.

But still she wanted to hear an unconditional
apology. It was what she deserved. It was what she
demanded.

'You don't have to have been there.' She stood
her ground determinedly, her eyes harshly sur-
veying his oddly shuttered face. 'You've known me
virtually all my life. You should know what I'm
like. You should know it's not in my nature to
behave as you described, offering my body to a
married man in return for supposed favours.'

She rose shakily to her feet. Her tone was ve-
hement with emotion. 'Forgive me, but you should
know me well enough to know I'm not a slut!'

Craig seemed to wince at that word. He took a
step towards her and reached out one hand to softly
touch her hair. 'Of course I know that. I never
meant to suggest...' He sighed and shook his head.
'Look, Fiona, I'm really sorry.'

But that still wasn't enough, though, at his touch,
she had shivered and felt the anger begin to melt
inside her. She took a deep breath and demanded,
'Does that mean that you don't believe what
Hamish said?'

His hand caressed her hair. He nodded. 'I guess
it does.' He smiled. 'You have your apology, Fiona.
Unequivocally, without any "ifs" or "buts".'

'You're quite sure about that?' She was loath to
trust him. Where on earth had such a sudden turn-
around come from? 'And does that mean that you

also believe,' she insisted, 'that what I told you about Hamish last night was true? That he's been pursuing me for months, driving me crazy? That that's the only reason I've been making mistakes at work?'

His hands were cupping her shoulders now, holding her at a distance, his eyes dark and earnest, poring into hers. 'Why didn't you do something about it?' he asked her softly. 'Why didn't you tell Doreen? That would have stopped him, as I'm sure you must have known.'

Oh, yes, she had known that. 'I threatened to tell Doreen. I threatened many times, but he knew I wouldn't do it.'

'How did he know that?'

'He knows I'm soft-hearted.' She pulled a wry, self-mocking face as she said it. 'He knew I didn't want to hurt her.'

Craig raised a questioning eyebrow. 'You didn't want to hurt Doreen? I was under the impression you didn't even like her!'

'I don't. But I feel sorry for her. And I know she cares for Hamish. I think she'd be devastated if anyone told her what he was like.'

A frown touched Craig's brow. He said nothing for a moment. The dark eyes seemed to scrutinise every line of her face. Then at last he conceded, 'I think you're probably right. Doreen's one of those women whose entire life revolves around her husband and family. Take that away from her and she'd probably fall apart.'

'That's why I said nothing.'

'And just put up with his bad behaviour?'

'I didn't put up with it. I did my best to put a stop to it. In the end, I thought he was bound to give up.'

There was a flicker behind Craig's eyes, a sudden tenseness about his mouth, as he told her now, 'Well, it's all over now. That's something I can absolutely guarantee.'

Fiona was suddenly aware that for the past couple of minutes neither of them had moved. She was still standing there, less than a foot away from him, his hands were still resting lightly on her shoulders, and, foolishly, she felt quite happy for her and Craig to stand there for ever, locked in a timeless, private little bubble.

She forced her mouth to move and said softly, 'I'm pleased to hear it.'

Craig smiled. 'And you accept my apology?'

'Now that it's a proper one, yes, I do.'

'Good.' He held her eyes. 'And now that that's out of the way, I have something very important to ask you...' As he paused, Fiona felt her stomach tighten strangely. Then he smiled. 'Shall we have dinner here, or shall we go out to a restaurant?'

For some silly reason her heart turned over. 'Oh, but I'm not staying,' she started to protest. 'I've said what I came for and now——'

'You're going home?' Craig cut in before she could finish. 'Is that what you were about to tell me?' He shook his head. 'In this weather, you're going nowhere—not until tomorrow morning at the very earliest.'

His grip around her shoulders tightened. He drew her towards him very gently. 'I don't think we should bother to go out to a restaurant. I think we should spend the evening right here.' As he said it, his lips seemed to softly brush her hair. She felt his breath warm and intimate against her scalp. 'What do you think?' he was asking now. 'Do you think that's a good idea?'

Fiona was aware of a hot, sweet melting within her, the like of which she had never known before.

She looked up into his face. 'Yes,' she said.

CHAPTER TEN

AND SO, to her own mild astonishment, Fiona stayed.

She stayed for dinner—steak and veg from the freezer, preceded by two bowls of steaming Scotch broth. She stayed for supper—more hot chocolate. And, finally, she stayed for the night.

It had all happened so naturally, as though it had been meant to, Fiona mused as she undressed in the bedroom next to Craig's. The only thing that had seemed at all strange about any of it was the fact that nothing like it had ever happened before.

They had known each other since they were children, yet this was the first time they'd spent time alone together. Just talking and laughing and doing everyday things, like grilling steaks and chopping onions.

'Fancy you being able to cook!' she'd observed with genuine amazement as, with the skill of a professional chef, he'd chopped the onion into slivers. 'I'm surprised you even know which end of the knife to use!'

Craig had glanced at her with amusement from beneath long lashes. 'If I say so myself, I'm a man of many talents. You haven't seen the half of it!'

She suspected she probably hadn't as, in the course of the evening, she learned many more unexpected things about him. 'Fancy you liking jazz!

I thought you were strictly into classical. My, you really are full of surprises!'

'And so are you.' He'd smiled back at her teasingly. 'I never thought for a moment that you possessed the good taste to appreciate the finer points of Dizzy Gillespie. Whoever would have thought we'd have common musical tastes?'

There had been other revelations, other shared passions—like Indian food and holidays in Italy—though in one or two areas they'd agreed to disagree.

'You'll never win me round to reading spy novels,' Fiona had assured him, laughing. 'I'll stick to more romantic sort of fare!'

She'd enjoyed it all immensely. There'd been an easiness between them and an air of simplicity about the evening that had made her wish it might go on for ever. And it might have if Craig hadn't suddenly glanced at his watch.

'Good grief!' he'd exclaimed. 'Would you believe it's after one o'clock? We'd better get to bed, or we'll never get up in the morning. We ought to be on the slopes by ten o'clock at the latest.'

'On the slopes? You must be joking! The only place I'm planning to go is back home!'

'You mean you'd come all this way, then not do any skiing?' Craig had smiled across at her, eyes wide and incredulous. 'Surely that would be a terrible waste of a journey?'

Fiona pulled a face. 'I can't even ski. I've only been on a pair of skis once in my life and I'm afraid I completely failed to get the hang of it.'

'In that case...' As she shrugged and paused for an instant, Fiona just knew what he was about to say next—that there was absolutely no point in her staying. And it was really quite appalling the way her heart sank.

But a moment later her spirits soared again as he continued, 'In that case, you're definitely staying. We'll arrange for you to have a couple of hours of lessons.'

'What am I supposed to wear? I don't have any ski things. I can scarcely go skiing dressed like this!'

'No problem. We can hire everything from the ski shop. We'll take care of it all first thing tomorrow morning.'

And now, as she pulled on a pair of Craig's friend's pyjamas and climbed into the comfy stripped-pine bed, she was looking forward with excitement to tomorrow. She could scarcely wait for morning to come.

But as she switched off the light and lay staring into the darkness, Fiona was aware of a flicker of uneasiness inside her. An uneasiness that was mingled with guilt.

Why was she suddenly so keen to learn to ski? The last time she had tried it she had hated every minute.

And what had happened to all her fine intentions to lay before Craig all the hurt and humiliation that he had inflicted on her over the years? She had referred to none of it. Once she'd gained his apology for what he'd said about her and Hamish, she'd obligingly let the subject drop.

It wasn't even as though she could claim that there'd been no opportunity. Over dinner Craig had presented her with the perfect opening.

As they'd pushed aside their steak-plates and he'd poured them both more wine, his expression had suddenly grown more serious. He'd looked into her eyes, his own eyes narrowing. 'I started to ask you this question once before... that evening at Hamish's when your car wouldn't start...'

He leaned towards her, making her heart flutter. 'You said something once that made me curious. I've always wondered exactly what you meant by it...' He paused. 'Why did you once say that you didn't know where I got the nerve from to look you in the face?'

Something froze inside Fiona. Abruptly, she had dropped her eyes away. 'That was nothing. Just something stupid.' She stared fixedly at the table-cloth. 'I don't even know what I meant by it myself.'

'Are you absolutely sure?'

'Absolutely.' She forced herself to meet his eyes. 'I must just have been annoyed with you about something.'

He'd seemed to accept that. 'Not a rare occurrence.' With a smile he raised his wine glass in a toast. 'Here's to better understanding. And to more evenings like this.'

Fiona had raised her glass to his gratefully, barely acknowledging, even to herself, the extent to which she had betrayed herself. In that moment it hadn't seemed to matter. All that had mattered was that the danger was past.

What danger? she asked herself now as she lay in the darkness. What had she been so afraid of in that moment?

She knew the answer and the answer shamed her. She had been afraid of spoiling the mood between them.

With a sigh she rolled over now and pressed her face into the pillow. She was being hard on herself, surely? That desire was not so shameful. After all, here she was, locked up all alone with him in this chalet, miles from home, with nowhere to run to. It would be foolish in such circumstances deliberately to embark on what was bound to be a long and acrimonious discussion. She would feel trapped, at his mercy, unable to escape. Surely she had been wise to postpone the confrontation?

And the skiing lessons? Had she been guided by wisdom there, too?

Why not? She frowned obstinately into her pillow. As Craig had said, it would be a waste to have come all this way and not take advantage of such a golden opportunity. And she *ought* to learn to ski. It was silly not to.

She felt much better for having rationalised away her guilty feelings. With a smile on her lips, Fiona drifted into sleep.

'So, how did it go? Have you conquered the nursery slopes yet?'

They were enjoying a late lunch in the mountaintop restaurant, seated at a table by the window with a panoramic view out over the ski slopes.

Fiona laughed and laid down her knife and fork. 'Not conquered, exactly, but I think I've got the hang of it. Another half a dozen lessons and I'll be almost as good as you!'

'Well, I must say, you looked as though you were enjoying yourself.' Craig smiled across at her, at her sparkling violet eyes and cheeks flushed pink with exertion—a pink almost as bright as the pink of the ski-suit she was wearing.

She smiled at him. Amazingly, she *had* enjoyed herself. Fancy me, she thought now, actually enjoying the snow!

'And from what I saw of your progress,' Craig continued, 'I'd say you've definitely got the hang of it.'

So, he had been watching her without her knowing. Foolishly, she found that immensely pleasing.

But she shrugged off the compliment and offered one of her own. 'I'm afraid I've a long way to go before I'm half as good as you, though. I saw you streaking down the mountainside while I was still struggling to master the ski-pull! I hate to admit it, but I was really impressed.'

That was putting it mildly. She had been more than impressed. At the sight of him flying down that mountainside, all grace and speed and easy elegance, a lump, inexplicably, had risen to her throat.

It was the beauty, the skill, the sheer professionalism of the performance, she had told herself impatiently, swallowing hard. She would have reacted

just the same had he been anyone else. It had
nothing to do with the fact that he was Craig.

As he smiled at her, she added, 'I envy you, you
know. It must be a truly wonderful feeling to hurtle
down a mountainside on two skis at such speed.'

'It is.' He smiled at her. 'Would you like to try
it?'

Fiona laughed. 'Maybe some day—a year or two
from now!'

'Why not right now? Why not this very afternoon? Why not just as soon as you've finished your
coffee?'

'Are you crazy?' Fiona blinked at him. 'Do you
want me to break a leg? I thought for once in our
lives we were supposed to be friends?'

She wished she hadn't said it. Her stomach tightened, as Craig sat back in his chair and gave her a
long look. That passing reference to their un-
friendly past was bound, she sensed, to spoil the
moment.

But he let it pass. He did not pick her up on it.
Instead, he said, 'If you really want to, I know a
way to give you a taste of what it feels like to come
down a mountain at that sort of speed. Without
breaking any limbs. I guarantee.'

'Really?' She was so grateful that he hadn't
picked up on her *faux pas* that she had only just
taken in what he was saying.

He nodded. 'Really.' Then he smiled, 'Trust me?'

She answered without thinking. 'Yes, I think so.'

'OK, then.' He was pushing back his seat. 'In
that case, I suggest we give it a go.'

It all happened so quickly that Fiona didn't have time to wonder what exactly she might have let herself in for. It was only once they were seated side by side on the chair-lift that she was suddenly seized by an attack of nerves.

'Are you sure this is a good idea? I'm just a beginner, remember.'

'Don't worry,' Craig winked at her. 'I'll look after you. You're about to have the thrill of your life.'

A moment later they were getting down from the chair-lift and heading for the top of the ski-run. Fiona blinked down nervously at the steep, icy slope disappearing between towering snow-clad fir trees, and felt the knot in her stomach tighten. How would she ever get down to the bottom in one piece?

'Here, give me those.' Craig was taking her ski-sticks and positioning himself so he was standing in front of her, his back towards her, only inches away. He glanced at her over his shoulder and instructed, 'Put your arms around my waist, let your body relax and just try to follow my body movements. 'Don't do anything yourself, just go with the flow.'

He threw her a wink. 'Are you ready? Let's just try it to the first bend and see how it goes.'

She was so stiff at first as they started to move that she was afraid she might cause them both to take a tumble. But, remembering his advice and somehow knowing she could trust him, she breathed slowly and forced herself to relax.

And it was like a miracle. Suddenly she was floating, her skis skimming smoothly over the snow's surface, effortlessly, like a bird in flight.

At the bend he slowed down. 'Are you OK, Fiona? You're not scared, are you? You wouldn't rather we stopped?'

'Definitely not. I'm not frightened in the slightest.'

'Good girl. Just hang on and stay relaxed.' He threw her a swift grin over his shoulder. 'You're doing great. See what a fine team we make?'

Fiona didn't have a chance to reflect on that remark, for the next instant she gasped as they began to gather speed—though it was a gasp of delight and excitement, not fear. He was right. This really was the thrill of her life.

She was laughing as she clung to him, feeling the wind in her face, her body glued to his, curving and moving with him, feeling the power of him almost as though it were a part of her, her heart flying as though it, too, had sprouted wings.

Fiona was breathless with exhilaration when they finally reached the bottom. She collapsed in a beaming heap as she released him. 'That was wonderful!' she declared. 'Can we do it again?'

Craig laughed. 'Are you serious?' He held out his hand to her. 'You really enjoyed it? You weren't scared at all?'

'Not in the slightest! It was fantastic!' She took his hand and let him pull her up.

'OK, if you want, we'll do it again.' He looked down into her eyes. 'Right now, if you like.'

There was something in his gaze that caused her heart to flutter. Suddenly, unexpectedly, something had changed.

'You did well, you know.' He had not released her hand. 'You have guts, young lady. But then I suppose I always knew that.'

Fiona wanted to look away, but her eyes remained fixed on him, just as her hand remained in his hand.

She heard herself say, 'I wasn't afraid because I trust you. I knew you wouldn't let me come to any harm.'

Craig smiled strangely. 'I'm extremely flattered. So, how come do I warrant such a display of total faith?'

Fiona was wondering that herself. She shrugged. 'I really don't know.'

She could hear the clamour of her heart ringing in her ears. And all at once the landscape all around her seemed frozen into a perfect, endless stillness. Suddenly she was locked into something she could not explain.

Craig was smiling. 'Don't you? Well, you really ought to know. After all these years, I reckon you ought to know why you trust me.'

Fiona swallowed as he bent briefly to undo the clips of his skis, then straightened again slowly. 'What are you doing?' she asked.

His eyes had never left her. He stepped free of his skis. 'I'm going to kiss you,' he told her, 'and there's no way I can kiss you when both of us are wearing skis.'

Fiona felt her heart constrict like a hot, pulsating ball. She could not speak and she could not move.

'Do you mind—my kissing you?'

He smiled as he said it, but it was not an ordinary smile; it was a smile such as she had never seen him smile before. A dark, smoky smile that set her pulses suddenly flickering and sent a wave of hot anxiety sweeping through her. Her ribs felt tight. She felt she might faint.

Then as he pulled away his gloves and reached out to touch her face, his touch as delicate as a whisper, Fiona could feel the blood surge in her head. She closed her eyes. She dared not look at him.

I'm a prisoner, she was thinking. In these skis I can't escape him. She felt his arms slide round her, drawing her against him. And her heart was in turmoil as she felt him bend towards her.

A moment later his lips were covering hers, his fingers were in her hair, his body pressed hard against her, and in her wildest dreams Fiona could never have imagined the total and instantaneous change that came over her.

An extraordinary charge of desire shot through her, a vivid, violent shock of pleasure and hunger, confusing and delicious, turning her heart over and leaving her raw and helpless with longing.

She could feel her heart thud like a huge drum inside her. The emotions driving through her were making her head spin. She gasped and leaned against him and was astonished to discover that her hands were on his shoulders, her fingers trickling through his hair.

Then he was drawing back a little, his dark eyes on her face. 'You have no idea how long I've wanted to do that.' He smiled. 'Would you mind if I did it again?'

Fiona smiled back at him. I would mind if you didn't! The words were in her eyes though she did not dare to speak them. And this time, as he bent to claim her with his lips, she was tilting her face towards him, eager, compliant. Never before had she been filled with such a desperate longing to kiss and be kissed by a man.

It was delicious, the hard, moist warmth of his mouth, devouring her, consuming her, sending shafts of yearning through her. And delicious, too, the way their bodies melded together. Beneath the heavy padded anorak she could feel his heart beating. She could almost imagine, as she pressed against him, the fiery touch of his naked skin.

His arms tight around her, he held her for a moment. 'What now?' he murmured against her cheek, making her shiver with anticipation. 'Do we do the run again or do we go straight back to the chalet? You tell me. I'm at your command.'

Fiona was tempted to say, 'Let's go back to the chalet.' She felt the dagger of desire go lancing through her. But she resisted. 'Let's just do the run once more,' she said instead. And, as he smiled and kissed her nose, she knew he had understood.

She had not been saying no to their return to the chalet and to what, almost inevitably, was bound to transpire there. To say no at that moment was quite beyond her. But she needed to collect herself before plunging into something so powerful, so terrifying, so beyond her control. The ski-run was simply a ploy to postpone the inevitable.

Craig knew that. She could sense it as they headed for the chair-lift. And he was enjoying the added *frisson* the delay lent the situation. The enforced reining in of the passion that raged within them simply added an extra bite.

They sat side by side like conspirators on the chair-lift, each electrically aware of the other, every tiny brush of thigh or shoulder an exquisite, almost unbearable, torture.

Then, without a word, they were heading for the ski-run, neither wasting a moment as they positioned themselves at the summit, both eager for that moment when they would plunge together from the edge, hurtling blindly into space. That thrilling, breath-taking, heart-stopping moment that would mark the beginning of the end of their torment.

Fiona's stomach tightened fiercely as she slipped her arms around his waist. Previously, it had not felt particularly intimate, but this time she could feel his body tense against her, as though in response to a sexual embrace. And her own body, as she clung to him, burned like a volcano. She could scarcely breathe for the tumult in her heart.

'Are you ready? Here we go!'

With a quick glance over his shoulder, a glance full of secret, sensual meaning, Craig was leaning forward, bending towards the incline, and an instant later, with a quick jerk of his body, they were off, heading unstoppably down into the abyss.

This time it was a thousand times more exciting than before. But it was not so much the thrill of their flight down the mountain that sent the blood rushing through Fiona's veins. The hiss of speeding skis, the rush of wind in her face, the heady sense of conquering the elements—these were all there, these were all a part of it, but they were no longer the focus of her exhilaration.

The excitement that possessed her had another source entirely. And its source was the man to whom she clung so fiercely, to whom at that moment her own body seemed welded, the man whose power was driving them forward, the man whose power she longed to unleash upon herself.

When they reached the bottom Fiona was shivering. Craig embraced her briefly, his lips brushing hers. But as his eyes gazed into hers, dark and smouldering, there was no need for questions, no need to ask, 'What next?'

Without a word he turned and led her back to the car park, to where the Land Rover was waiting to take them down to the chalet. Her heart on fire, her body fluid with desire, scarcely daring to look at him, Fiona followed him.

CHAPTER ELEVEN

THE journey back to the chalet in the gathering darkness had a distant, almost unreal feeling.

In her mind Fiona was already there. All that was about to unfold there was already unfolding in her imagination. Every inch of her being throbbed and burned.

They went through all the motions, just like yesterday. Craig propped his skis, and hers, in the vestibule, then proceeded to divest himself of boots and anorak. Fiona did the same, hanging up her hat and gloves. Her heart was pounding. She dared not even glance at him.

Through in the hallway, the warmth enveloped her, and she remembered how, yesterday, it had felt so wonderful. Today it hardly seemed to matter. No warmth could match the fire that burned within.

At the doorway that led to the sitting-room she hesitated. Should she, she wondered, suggest making cocoa? Or should she, first, go and switch on the big gas fire?

Craig made the decision for her, and the decision was neither. In that moment of hesitation he had come up behind her. She almost started as she felt his arms slip around her.

He pulled her to him, so that her back curved against him, so that she could feel the sharp jut of his hardness, and with a sigh he buried his face in her hair.

Then he was turning her to face him, his arms encircling her, his breath jagged with desire as his head bent over her and, hungrily, his lips sought hers.

It was an urgent, fierce, almost violent kiss. They came together like an explosion. It felt similar, Fiona thought, to that moment on the mountain when they had tipped over the edge and hurtled into space. And, as at that moment, she could sense there was no going back.

As he kissed her, he was pulling her top from her ski-pants and simultaneously leading her through the living-room door. She gasped as his hand made contact with her naked flesh, then shivered as without preamble he pushed aside her bra and greedily caressed her breasts with his fingers.

She felt her breasts swell and harden, the nipples thrusting against him.

Still kissing her and caressing her, he had drawn her to the fireside, switched on the fire, then pulled her gently down beside him on to the big soft sheepskin rug.

'Fiona, Fiona...'

His voice was rough and ragged as he peeled away her top and tossed aside the bra, snatching cushions from the nearby sofa to lay beneath her head. Then, as she relaxed back against them, her whole body tingling, he was tugging away his own tight-fitting sweater, then pressing against her, his nakedness making her shiver.

'You have no idea how much I want you.' He kissed her face, her shoulders, her breasts, teasing the thrusting nipples with the tip of his tongue, sending an ache of desire, like molten fire, through her loins.

Then he was peeling away her ski-pants, stripping her naked, pausing to caress with sensuous fingers her stomach, her flanks, the trembling flesh of her thighs.

And, shamelessly, Fiona was reaching for him, her fingers tugging at the waistband of his ski-pants, as, breathing fast, he wriggled free of them, finally to fall against her, hard with desire.

He wrapped her in his arms and held her close for a moment, his eyes looking down at her, raw with passion. He kissed her on the lips, his hands caressing her. 'This is a dream,' he murmured. 'A dream come true.'

Then, with a sigh, he was bending over her, igniting her skin with his fingers, then her whole body tensed, her heart thrashing inside her, as he leaned to take one hot, hard nipple between his lips.

Every inch of her was clamouring for him as he held her firmly, strumming with his tongue, his teeth gently teasing her. And at that moment it seemed to her that nothing in the world could prevent the inevitable bonding of their bodies. She reached for him hungrily. She would not let it!

But then, his voice a whisper, he murmured against her ear, 'I always knew you'd be mine. One day. Eventually. Even back in the days when we were both children.'

The words were like a bullet, driving into her brain, making her stop in her tracks and slam on the brakes. In an instant she was transported to another time, another place, away from the intimacy and warmth of that fireside back to the cold, hostile wilderness of her childhood.

She tried to mask the reaction, to thrust it from her, to push away the chill that had swept over her flesh. With a small shiver she clung to him, her face pressed against his chest. It doesn't matter, she told herself. I still want him. Don't deny me!

But he had caught that small reaction. He drew her softly against him. 'Don't worry, I'm not trying to push you into anything. I've waited long enough, I can wait a while longer. We don't have to be in such a hurry.'

He kissed her face and pushed back her hair gently. 'Just being here with you like this is more than enough for starters.' He caressed her softly. 'We've plenty of time for all the rest.'

Fiona remained very still, lying with her face against him, and at that moment she could not even begin to sort out the maelstrom of emotions that went tearing through her. Bitter disappointment, shock and horror, and a sense of confusion and fearful anguish that were almost more than she could bear.

In that instant she hated him and resented him, yet desired him still with a ferocity that tore at her. His arms around her seemed both to threaten and protect her. The touch of him froze her, yet consumed her with fire.

What's happening to me? She almost sobbed the words out loud. Her whole world, all at once, seemed to be falling down around her.

Somehow Fiona managed to get through the rest of the evening. And on one level, at least, it wasn't really difficult.

Craig seemed unaware of the tumult within her. He didn't seem to notice that she was acting rather oddly.

Perhaps, Fiona wondered, he had simply put down to embarrassment her sudden slightly distant demeanour? Perhaps he had concluded that she was modestly regretting those moments of passion by the fireside?

The truth was rather different. She had tried to regret them. She had spoken to herself firmly and told herself she had behaved shamefully. But regret was not forthcoming. She felt no shame whatsoever. On the contrary, each time she thought about it her skin tingled deliciously.

She had also striven with an equal lack of success to switch off the relaxed way she felt in his company. She'd tried to freeze the easy warmth she suddenly felt towards him. She'd struggled not to respond to his conversation, and, above all, not to laugh at his jokes.

But her efforts had got her precisely nowhere. As they prepared dinner that evening and watched the TV news, she felt oddly removed from her own jumbled emotions. It was so easy just to get along with him. It suddenly seemed to come naturally. To have done anything else would have required a huge effort.

She had made an effort, though. She'd tried to cut their stay short.

Before dinner she'd suggested, 'Oughtn't we to get back home tonight? After all, it's Monday to-morrow. We have to get back to work.'

He'd smiled. 'Don't worry, I won't complain if you're late. In fact, I won't even complain if you take the morning off.' Then, as she'd tried to pull a frown of protest, he'd added, 'It's much safer to make the journey in daylight. It's snowing again and the roads could be bad. Besides,' he'd pointed out, winking at her, 'we have to hand in your ski things to the hire shop. We could have done it this afternoon, if we'd thought about it, but I guess we had other things on our minds.'

Fiona did blush then, though it was a blush of remembered pleasure. And she was to blush again later when he kissed her goodnight.

Not out of confusion, for the confusion had left her the instant she had felt his lips press against hers. She had blushed for the flames that had leapt up inside her, for the urge to press against him and explore his naked flesh—though not out of shame, but rather for the excitement of the sensation. It scorched her cheeks and every inch of her flesh.

But he had been discreet, he had not pressed her further, though he must have sensed the ache of desire that sprang from her. He was being true to his promise to take things easy. What was it he had said? 'We have time enough for all of that.'

A moment later, as she closed her bedroom door, Fiona was deeply grateful for his thoughtful restraint. For, instantly, all her confusion come rushing back in on her.

When she was around him it was easy. In his arms there was no problem. But the instant she stepped back, the instant he was no longer with her, her head could scarcely contain the tangled emotions within her.

And still she could find no answer to the question that twisted round and round in her brain.

What's happening to me? What's happening to me?

Next morning they were up just after seven and on the road by half-past eight.

To Fiona's relief, few words passed between them, as they took turns in the bathroom, then snatched a quick breakfast, before climbing into their separate cars.

Craig seemed perfectly relaxed and just as friendly as yesterday, but Fiona was growing more confused by the minute. Suddenly, she no longer knew how to react to him. His smiles made her heart jump uneasily within her. When he touched her, even unintentionally, she could feel her flesh burn.

I have to get away from him. I have to be alone. I need time to think and unravel my emotions. Otherwise, I shall explode!

As they were leaving the house, he paused for a moment. 'I'll lead the way. You stay close behind me. Just bang your horn if you have any problems.'

Then his expression became more serious. 'We'll have dinner together this evening. I'd make it lunch, but I'm going to be far too busy.' He smiled and reached out to brush back a tendril of her hair. 'I think you and I have a lot to talk about.'

Fiona nodded ambiguously. Dinner was a long way away. Between now and then, perhaps she'd have straightened herself out.

The journey back to Inverairnie went mercifully smoothly, though the road in parts was as slippery as glass. Fiona kept close behind the big Land Rover, half wishing every time it disappeared round a corner that it might vanish into the snowy mists for ever. Yet one time when she did momentarily lose sight of it, and it seemed that her wish had unexpectedly come true, she was assailed by such a storm of uncontrollable panic that her heart seemed almost to stop dead inside her.

Without him, I shall be lost! The thought drove through her. Without him I simply cannot survive!

But then she spotted him again and in shame and relief she clutched at the driving-wheel and sighed a trembling sigh. And, again, the question returned to torment her: *What's happening to me? What's happening to me?*

On the outskirts of Inverairnie he drew into the side of the road, climbed out of the Land Rover and called to her as she came alongside him, 'This is where we part company. I'll see you at the office. And remember to keep yourself free for dinner.'

Again, Fiona responded with an ambiguous nod. Then with a brief wave she was driving past him and heading at speed for Bonnie Braes.

*   *   *

Fiona was relieved that there was no one at home. Iris—whom she had phoned earlier to tell her to expect her—had left a note in the kitchen to say she'd gone out shopping.

She shook her head as she hurried upstairs to shower and change. For almost all of her life Iris had been her confidante, but not even to Iris could she confide her inner turmoil. How could she confide what she could not understand?

Yet, thankfully, now that Craig was no longer around, the tumult inside her was gradually receding. In its place a kind of numbness was taking hold of her. As she changed into black trousers and a red silk blouse, she was aware that she was moving like an automaton. And not thinking at all. She dared not think.

It was just after eleven-thirty when Fiona set off for the office, her mind steadfastly set on matters of business. It was like a balm to her embattled brain to know she had a busy day ahead of her. Work. That was all she could cope with at the moment.

But as she turned into the car park at Birnam Wood Repro, in an instant all thoughts of work were dashed from her head. She drew to a halt, her heart frozen into stillness, and stared in dismay at the mud-spattered Land Rover that was parked half out of sight in one corner.

It had caught her eye instantly, in spite of its position. It was Craig's Land Rover. The one he had hired. And right now he was seated in the front seat, his back to her, quite unaware of her presence, head bent, arms locked around a red-haired girl.

A girl she recognised. Celia Strachan, an ex-employee.

A clawing pain went through her, filling every corner. Tears of shock and shame rose up in her eyes. Yet, in that same instant, as all the numbness was driven from her, miraculously her brain seemed to clear.

This was the real Craig whom she was seeing at this moment, the Craig who, behind that beguiling façade, was all dishonesty, deceit and lies. This was the true Craig, the Craig who used people, who cared not a damn about how badly he might hurt them.

And, above all, her heart told her, this was the Craig she had always known, the Craig who despised her, who had always hated her. Her once and for always implacable enemy.

Somehow, she parked her car and made it into the office. Her legs felt like rubber. Her heart was still thundering. But, suddenly, she understood everything.

Craig's unexpected apology up at the chalet, knowing what had followed, suddenly made sense. He'd been stringing her along, taking advantage of her foolishness. What he had been doing, quite simply, was amusing himself.

She cursed herself angrily as she sat behind her desk and tried to concentrate on the files of figures before her. She ought to have known. Doreen had warned her about the girl, but she had barely registered the warning.

She smiled to herself wryly. At that stage it hadn't mattered. At that stage nothing had been further from her mind than romance!

Restlessly, she shifted in her seat. Perhaps he and the girl had fallen out for some reason and that was why she hadn't accompanied him on his skiing trip. Whatever the reason, he'd found himself all alone, devoid of amenable female company... until, oh, so conveniently, she herself had come along!

Fiona shivered. That was why he had offered her his fake apology—in order to bewitch her into spending the weekend with him. Hadn't he once told her how he hated to be without a woman? And any woman was better than no woman at all!

Nausea welled up inside her. How easily she'd been duped! And how close she'd come to allowing him to make love to her! She dropped her head in her hands. Far more horrifying than that was the memory of how desperately she had wanted him.

She had two choices now. She could refuse to speak to him and make it very plain that she wanted nothing more to do with him. Or she could be bold and confront him and tell him what she thought of him. Of the two choices, she definitely preferred the latter.

By one o'clock, however, he had still not shown up. He had probably gone off somewhere with the girl, Celia Strachan. Fiona never left her desk—she could not have eaten anyway. Like a tiger she sat with her office door half open, waiting for him to appear, ready to pounce.

And then, just after four, she heard footsteps down the corridor, firm, striding footsteps that she recognised instantly. A moment later Craig swept swiftly past her door, jaw set, eyes glancing neither to right nor to left.

Fiona sat very still until she heard his office door close. Then, grimly determined, she rose to her feet and made her way on swift strides down the corridor.

She tapped sharply, twice, and pushed his office door open. Then she stepped inside. 'May I have a word?'

He had the phone in his hand. He'd been punching in a number. He glanced up at her, frowning. 'Would you mind coming back later?'

Fiona felt perversely grateful for that unwelcoming opening. It steeled her resolve and added relish to her mission.

'Yes, I'm afraid I would.' She closed the door behind her and, very deliberately, took another step towards him. 'What I want to say I want to say now.'

He frowned and sighed and laid down the receiver. 'I see.' He paused, his eyes flicking over her. 'So, what is it that you have, so urgently, to tell me?'

There was a distant look about him, an air of preoccupation, in spite of the smile that briefly touched his lips. He had already forgotten what had passed between them yesterday. It had meant nothing at all to him. A way of passing the time.

Fiona felt her fists clench with hurt and anger. He had simply used her for his amusement. Again.

She said in a cold tone, 'About this evening...I'm afraid I won't be free for dinner.'

'Something come up, has it?' He scarcely even looked at her. Once more his eyes were fixed on the phone.

'No, nothing's come up.' Her fists were clenched so tightly it felt as though her nails were cutting into her flesh. 'I've changed my mind. I've gone off the idea. Besides,' she added acidly, 'I'm sure you've got better things to do.'

She should not have said that. It sounded weak and peevish. But he did not deny the unhappy allegation. Instead, he simply shrugged. 'Some other time, then? Perhaps we can fix up something for tomorrow?'

His casual, offhand tone cut and enraged her. With an effort Fiona swallowed back her seething emotions.

'No, not tomorrow. In fact, not ever.' She had the satisfaction of seeing him glance up at her then. 'There's really no need for us to go through the motions just because we had a couple of kisses on the hearthrug. They meant nothing—to either of us—and, now that the weekend's over, I suggest we just get back to normality. You don't like me and I don't like you, and neither of us wants to endure having dinner with the other.' She smiled a cynical smile. 'There's no point in playing games.'

'Absolutely not. We're both a little old for that.' He had leaned back in his chair, dark eyes narrowed, scrutinising her. And there was an edge of mocking humour in his tone as he added, 'Still, you surprise me, I must say. I hadn't realised you were just playing.'

It was an effort to stifle the blush that rose to her cheeks. Fiona dug her nails fiercely into the palms of her hands. If only she *had* just been playing! If only she were capable of such a thing!

She forced a stiff smile. 'Both of us were playing. And it was you, needless to say, who set up our little game...' As he raised a curious eyebrow, she hurried on and put to him, 'That apology of yours...when you said you didn't believe that story Hamish told you about him and me...' She took a deep breath. 'You didn't mean that, did you?'

It struck her, as she waited for him to answer, that she could scarcely really blame him if he believed Hamish's story. After yesterday's little episode, which she had just claimed had been only a game to her, why should he not believe that she had behaved likewise with his brother, baring her breasts at him in an effort to seduce him?

So she was frankly astonished when he answered, 'As a matter of fact, I did mean it. Why should I say it if I didn't?'

Could she believe him? Fiona narrowed her eyes at him. 'And do you still believe it?' she demanded.

'Why would I change my mind?' The dark eyes were piercing. 'I'm really not in the habit of doing so with such frequency.'

'In that case...' She held her breath. Now she would test him. 'In that case, you should also still believe what I told you about how Hamish has been pestering me, making sexual advances, and that that's the reason why I've been making mistakes?' Her eyes flickered a challenge at him. 'Is that the case?'

Craig held her eyes a moment. 'Why do you doubt me? Why do you feel it necessary to demand these assurances?'

Fiona almost laughed out loud. 'I wonder?' she taunted. Then she flashed him a look. 'Don't try to change the subject. Just answer my questions, if you don't mind.'

'I told you already...' his tone was low and measured, the tone of a man who was rapidly losing patience '...I'm not in the habit of changing my mind every five minutes.'

'That means you believe what I told you?'

'It would appear so.'

'What I told you about Hamish?'

'What you told me about Hamish.'

'Then you can't believe any longer that I'm incompetent? You can't believe that I deserve to be thrown out of the company?' Suddenly she was floundering. She had not expected this reaction. Suddenly she seemed to have lost the focus of her anger. She clenched her fists tighter. 'You admit your brother is a liar?'

The expression on Craig's face had never altered. That distant, remote look still darkened his eyes. Only his clipped tone of voice betrayed his mounting impatience, as he informed her, 'I withdraw all allegations of incompetence. I see no need for you to step down from your current position.'

'And what about your brother? Is he to get away with all the lies he told about me? Is that what's to happen? Is he to get away scot-free?'

Craig looked back at her unblinkingly. 'I intend to have a word with my brother.'

'A *word*? That's terrific! I might have known that's all that would happen! Hamish gets a ticking off from big brother and everything continues as before!'

Her voice had risen to a hysterical screech, the anger, the hurt, the resentment inside her suddenly too ferocious to control. She saw Craig lean forward and start to rise to his feet. He was saying something, but she was no longer listening.

She continued to screech at him. 'That's it! I'm quitting! I've had enough of you and your brother and Birnam Wood Repro! If this is the way the company's to be run, I no longer wish to have any part of it!' Her eyes flashed like firecrackers. 'You can have my share whenever you want it! Buy me out! That's what we both want!' She flounced towards the door. 'I've had more than I can stomach!'

It was only as she was fleeing out to the car park, pulling her hastily grabbed camel coat around her, that it suddenly struck Fiona that, quite subconsciously, this final, irrevocable break was what she'd been planning all day.

And the relief was enormous that at last the bonds were broken. The bonds that had held her a prisoner for so long, and that had inflicted upon her such pain and misery.

She was free at last. Free of the scourge of her childhood. Free for ever of Craig Campbell.

CHAPTER TWELVE

ONLY it was not quite as simple and easy as that. For in that moment, when she had flung her resignation at Craig in a final, desperate effort to shed the shackles of the past, Fiona had understood with terrifying clarity what the true nature of those shackles had always been.

It was not that she had been bound to him by Birnam Wood Repro, or in the past by her father's association with his father. These were not the ties that had allowed his influence to linger, insidiously, relentlessly blighting her life. The ties, the shackles, that had bound her to him—and that, in spite of her gesture, bound her still—were of a very different nature.

A sick horror drove her.

She loved Craig Campbell. She had loved him every second of her life.

Yet she could not accept that. Perhaps, once, she had loved him—once, when she'd been too young to know any better. But surely she had overcome that? She had not loved him for years, and surely she did not love him now? Surely she hated him, with every fibre of her soul?

She drove and drove, as it grew dark all around her, not knowing where she was going, following road signs at random, eyes fixed blindly on the road, as though, by putting miles between the two of them, she could wipe out the truth of that shattering revelation.

But it followed her like a shadow, it sat perched there on her shoulder. Ignoring it, even denying it, could not make it go away.

Tears streamed down her face, though she was barely aware of them. Had she really always been in love with Craig Campbell? Had that childhood madness never really died? No wonder her psyche had suppressed these dangerous emotions and transformed them into something she could handle—hate.

A shudder went through her. Hate had been her protection, her armour, her shield against the annihilation of her soul. Hating him, she had suffered, but how much greater the suffering if she had continued to look at him through the defenceless eyes of love. She would never have survived. She would have been crushed beneath his malice. Her heart, long ago, would have been ground into dust.

And now? The question froze her. What would happen to her now? Now that she was revealed? Now that the mask was torn away?

I shall simply have to learn genuinely to hate him. She gritted her teeth. That shouldn't be hard.

Yet she could not contain the great wave of despair that all at once engulfed her heart. The car slewed to the roadside and juddered to a halt, as with a sob that almost tore her in two she dropped her head against the steering-wheel and let her agony pour out.

*　　*　　*

Finally, the storm in her heart abated. Swollen-faced and exhausted, Fiona sat for a while, staring unseeingly into the cold, snowy night.

Iris will be wondering where I've got to, it suddenly occurred to her. She glanced at her watch. It was almost eight o'clock. I'd better get back and let her know I'm all right.

And that was when, as she tried to turn on the ignition, she realised she was completely out of petrol. She sighed, but she was too numb from the storm of weeping to feel anything other than mild irritation. In a way, she almost welcomed this small inconvenience. It was a diversion. It stopped her thinking about Craig.

She had to walk two miles to the nearest filling-station, then, with a borrowed container filled with petrol, walk all the back again in the driving snow. She was cold, she was wet, she felt physically exhausted, but her frozen face and near-solidified fingers helped to keep her mind off the agony in her heart. More than the prospect of collapsing and dying of exposure she dreaded the moment when she would have to face that.

At last, with a full tank, she was heading back to Inverairnie, faintly astonished to discover that she had ended up in Ballater, more than halfway along the road to Inverness.

'I'll be home in a couple of hours,' she'd advised a worried Iris when she'd phoned from the petrol station before setting off. 'If you feel like an early night, don't bother waiting up.'

She smiled wryly to herself now as she headed homewards. Iris probably would wait up. She'd

sounded worried. And, in a way, Fiona would be
glad to see a friendly face, though she was far from
ready yet to confide her agony to another. Even to
Iris. She must face it first herself.

It was with mixed feelings that she drove into a
deserted Inverairnie and headed towards Bonnie
Braes. She had always loved this place, but now she
must leave it. Sell up the house and her share of
the business, move somewhere new and make a
fresh start. There was no alternative, if she were
not to go mad.

For she must never see Craig again, nor even hear
his name spoken. She must never think of him. She
must blot him from her memory. And here in
Inverairnie that would be impossible. Here he was
everywhere. With every step he would follow her.

The house lights were on as she turned into
Bonnie Braes and parked the car at the side of the
house. Dear Iris, no doubt, was waiting up for her,
even though it was after ten o'clock and well past
her bedtime.

Fiona hurried towards the front door. I'll just
have a quick word with her, reassure her that I'm
OK, then take myself off to bed.

To bed, but not to sleep. A sense of dread un-
curled within her. She saw a future of sleepless black
nights stretch out ahead of her. By day she could
keep busy and hold the spectres at bay. But in the
lonely, merciless hours after midnight, she knew for
certain, that would not be so easy.

She stepped into the hallway and made an effort
to compose herself, pinning a tight, brave smile on
her face.

'Iris, I'm home!' She dropped her bag on the hall table, pulled off her gloves and glanced at her reflection in the hall mirror.

And then a voice behind her spoke.

'You look absolutely ghastly. And where the devil have you been?'

He was standing in the drawing-room doorway, his hands thrust into his trouser pockets, his image reflected in the mirror. Fiona felt herself freeze. The smile melted from her face. She stared back at him, suddenly unbearably full of pain.

'I've been waiting here for hours.' Craig stepped into the hallway. 'Do you mind telling me where the devil you've been?'

To hell and back. But she did not say that. She dropped her eyes from the mirror, her back still towards him. 'Where's Iris?' she demanded. 'Is she waiting up for me?'

'She would be if I hadn't told her to get off to bed.'

Suddenly, he was standing right behind her. She felt his hand touch her arm, causing her to flinch involuntarily.

Fiona whirled round defensively. 'What are you doing here?'

He was standing very still, his dark eyes on her, so familiar, so handsome, such a powerful presence that Fiona almost could not bear to look at him. Tears scalded her eyes. It was utterly shaming just how much, in spite of everything, she adored him.

In a quiet voice he said, 'You ought to get out of that coat. It's wet and you look frozen. Here, let me help you.'

Again, she flinched away from him as he reached out towards her. 'You haven't answered my question. What are you doing here?'

He did not answer immediately. The dark eyes fixed her, and there was an intensity in that gaze that made her shiver.

'What's the matter?' he challenged, his gaze never flickering. 'Did you think I lacked the nerve to look you in the face?'

In spite of her inner anguish, Fiona smiled wryly. So, he had still not forgotten her accusation!

Undoing her camel coat, she stepped away from him. 'You have the nerve for anything. I ought to know that.' As she slipped the coat from her shoulders, she shivered. 'Whatever you've come for, I wish you'd leave now. I'm really not in the mood to talk.'

'That's a pity.' Without moving, he continued to watch, as she hung her coat in the cloakroom, then kicked off her boots. 'You see,' he added, as she threw him a harsh look, 'I won't be leaving until I've finished what I've come for.'

A surge of anger drove through her, momentarily displacing her misery. 'This is my house! You'll leave when I tell you to! Don't think you can just walk in here and start making threats!'

Then, as a thought suddenly occurred to her, she folded her arms across her chest and narrowed her eyes at him disdainfully. 'If you've come to check up on whether or not I was serious about getting out of Birnam Wood Repro and selling off my share, set your mind at rest. I've never been more serious. It's yours whenever you're ready to hand over the money.'

Craig's dark eyes looked right through her. 'That doesn't interest me at the moment. To gain that assurance is not what I'm here for.'

'Then what are you here for?' There was something about his demeanour, a weight of intensity in his eyes, that scared her. She folded her arms more firmly over her bosom. 'What is it that you want of me?' she demanded.

'An answer. An explanation——' He broke off suddenly. 'Can we go next door?' He gestured towards the sitting-room. 'Standing out here in the hall isn't really conducive to conversation.'

All the more reason to stay there! Fiona eyed him flintily. 'Maybe I don't feel like conversation. Maybe I don't feel like being told what to do in my own home!'

'I think what you feel like is taking the weight off your feet.' He smiled as he said it, making her poor heart turn over. 'Come on, let me pour you a glass a brandy.' He smiled again. 'Unless you'd prefer a cup of cocoa?'

Something buckled inside her as he held her eyes a moment. Suddenly, she was transported back to the chalet at Aviemore. Pain washed through her. Just for a moment she could not speak.

He had seen her weakness and now he proceeded to exploit it. 'Brandy, then.' He was striding towards the sitting-room. 'Come on. The sooner you do as I ask, the sooner you'll be rid of me.'

She could easily have turned around and fled upstairs. She almost did so. But she knew he would follow her. She could sense his determination. He would not leave until he had finished with her.

As she stepped into the sitting-room, he was standing by the bar, pouring a generous measure into one of the balloon brandy glasses. He handed it to her as she seated herself in an armchair by the fire. 'There,' he smiled. 'That ought to warm you.'

Fiona took the glass without looking at him, cupping her hands around it, leaning towards the fire. She was aware of him seating himself in the sofa opposite her. She could feel his eyes on her, burning through her.

At last, he spoke. 'I'll come straight to the point. As I said, I've come here looking for an explanation. I want you to explain that remark you made to me...'

He paused. 'This is the third time I've requested an explanation. The first time—that night I came here—we ended up fighting. Then I asked you the other evening at the chalet, but you wriggled out of it without giving me an answer. This time I won't let you off the hook so easily...'

His eyes were still on her, though she had not turned to look at him. 'You know what I'm talking about. I'm talking about your remark that you were surprised that I should have the nerve to look you in the face.'

Fiona spun round then. 'You can't be serious? You know exactly what I meant by that!'

'If I did, I wouldn't be here.'

'You're a liar, Craig Campbell!'

'Perhaps I am, but in this instance I'm not lying. I quite genuinely haven't a clue what you meant by that remark.'

Fiona turned away, her anger almost choking her. How dared he have the nerve to sit here in her sitting-room and spout such blatant insincerities? Did he have no respect for her? Did he take her for an idiot?

She turned to look at him, rabid with fury. 'Very well, then.' She drove the words at him as if they were ice-picks. 'Since your memory so conveniently fails you, allow me to refresh it for you.' She sat back in her chair and took a mouthful of her brandy. 'I hope you're not in any hurry? This might take a little time.'

She would give it to him without mercy, chapter and verse. She would spare him nothing of his wicked, evil past!

He looked back at her unblinkingly. 'Take your time. I'm in no hurry.'

'OK, let's begin with the adoption revelation...' Glaring at him, hating him, Fiona launched straight in. 'That's as good a place as any to start.'

The task of refreshing his conveniently defective memory was like shedding a great weight from her soul. Her voice tense with emotion, Fiona reminded him of what had happened that day so long ago. How Hamish had jeered at her and told her she was adopted, how Craig himself later had smilingly commented that she'd get over it, that she had had to find out some time.

She told him, too, about how he had ruined her confirmation, and reminded him of all the other occasions when, using his younger brother as his mouthpiece, he had deliberately blighted her life.

'You even convinced me for a while that my parents didn't love me! You told Hamish you overheard my father say so to your mother! You ruined my childhood!' She was suddenly close to tears. 'I'll never forgive you for that! Never!'

Fiona turned her face away from him. She could not look at him. All at once her entire body was trembling uncontrollably.

Craig did not speak. He had not moved a muscle. And there was something eerie about his stillness and his silence.

Then he rose to his feet slowly. 'I need a drink,' Fiona heard him murmur. Then he was walking on long strides across the carpet. A moment later she heard the clink of glasses.

There was another long silence, oddly unnerving. Then she heard him breathe deeply. He said in a low voice, 'Do you know what I did this afternoon, after you stormed out of the office?'

Fiona half turned to look at him. He was standing with his back to her, very still, staring into his whisky glass.

'I have no idea. And I'm not really interested.' Her voice still trembled with emotion. Was that all he had to say about what she'd just told him?

'I went to see Hamish.' It was as though she hadn't spoken. He knocked back his drink and turned abruptly to face her. 'I've removed him from his position as managing director of the company.'

Fiona blinked. 'Why did you do that?' And why, she was wondering, was he suddenly acting so strangely?

Craig laid down his empty glass and walked slowly towards her. He looked pale. His eyes seemed to burn from his head.

He took a deep breath. 'Do you really need to ask? A man who falsifies company records and bribes his secretary to play along with him, a man who lies and invents stories about a senior member of staff in an effort to discredit her and squeeze her out of the company is not a man who deserves to hold any position of authority...'

There was pain written clearly on his face as he continued, 'And if, on top of all of that, he is also given to sexual harassment of female members of his staff, then he is not a man I wish to employ in my company at any level.'

Fiona could scarcely believe what she was hearing. Such a heartfelt, damning indictment of Hamish coming from the lips of his brother! This was something she had thought she would never live to hear!

'When did you find out that he'd been lying and faking documents? And how did you find out?' she wondered aloud.

'I began to suspect...' His eyes were as hard as boulders. 'I decided to tackle his secretary, Sheena. This afternoon she finally told me everything.'

There was a moment of silence, then Fiona had another question. 'When you were talking about your brother's penchant for sexual harassment, you said female members of staff—*members*, plural.

Was there someone else at the company he was harassing?'

Craig nodded. 'Celia Strachan. She's been trying to see me since I came up to Inverairnie. She finally managed to catch me in the car park this morning.' He shook his head grimly. 'Poor kid was in a real state. Distraught. She couldn't handle it. She told me she'd left rather than put up with it. But she needs her job back. That's why she came to me.'

He broke off with a half-smile. 'What you said last night was right. He was harassing you in the hope that, with that added to everything else, you'd eventually break and leave the company. That was what happened with poor Celia—though with her that hadn't been his intention—and he thought he could repeat the formula with you.'

A strange look crossed his eyes. 'But he misjudged you. You're not weak like Celia. You put up a fight.'

The compliment warmed her like unexpected sunshine. And at the same time Fiona was aware of a ridiculous surge of pleasure to learn the truth about what had been happening in the car park. He had been comforting Celia, not seducing her!

Yet it almost broke her heart that that should actually still matter to her. After all she had just a moment ago finished recounting to him, all the suffering that over the years he had so callously inflicted, how was it possible that she could go on loving him?

She pushed these thoughts from her. 'I wasn't so courageous. And I know how she feels. It's not an easy thing to handle.' Then she added, oddly moved by the pain that dulled his eyes, 'It must have been quite a shock for you to discover what Hamish has been getting up to.'

'It was.' He sighed. 'And I only knew the half of it.' He took a step towards her and, quite unexpectedly, reached down and took the brandy glass from her hand. He laid it to one side, then surprised her further by bending down in front of her, on his haunches, to look up at her.

Craig took her hands in his, his dark eyes earnest. 'If you never believe another word I ever say to you, I want you to believe what I'm about to say to you now.' He paused before demanding softly, 'Will you?'

Her heart was beating strangely. Fiona nodded. 'I can't promise,' she told him, 'but I'll try.'

His hands held her hands tightly. 'What you told me just a moment ago shocked me more than you can ever know. If you had told me just a couple of days ago, I would never have believed you, but a couple of days ago the scales had not yet fallen from my eyes.'

With a shudder he continued, 'All those stories you told me...it was like a nightmare having to listen to them. My brother was never my mouthpiece. I knew nothing of what you've just told me. In fact, what you've just told me has turned upside-down all that I believed for years.'

He frowned, his dark eyes burning. 'I believed *you* were evil. Heartless, vindictive—as you must have believed of me. Hamish used to come to me with these awful stories of the terrible, cruel things you'd said and done to him. I never intervened.

You were younger than he was and I felt he ought to be able to stand up for himself. But I believed him. Utterly. I could see no reason not to. I never thought for a moment that I had a liar for a brother.'

Fiona stared at him, stunned. Could what he was telling her be true? Could Hamish have been playing a double game all these years?

But she was being gullible. She shook her head impatiently. 'You're making this up. You weren't innocent. I remember the way you sat there smirking after Hamish had told me I was adopted. "She'll get over it," you said. "She had to find out some time." Go on!' she challenged him. 'How do you explain that?'

Craig leaned back on his heels a little and paused for a moment. 'OK,' he admitted. 'I knew he'd been up to something . . .'

'And you found it amusing that he should have just shattered my whole world?' Tears sprang to Fiona's eyes. 'How could you? How could you?'

His grip on her hands tightened. He leaned towards her. 'I had no idea he'd told you you were adopted. I believed it was something else entirely.' He smiled a rueful smile. 'What Hamish told me was that he had just told you the facts of life. That was why I was smirking. I was thirteen years old. Thirteen-year-old boys smirk about sex.

'Good God!' he scowled, suddenly angry. 'If I had even suspected what he'd really been up to, I swear to you I would have torn him to pieces. I would never have allowed him to hurt you like that!'

He caught her hands to his lips and kissed them softly, glancing up earnestly into her eyes. 'And all the other stuff. How could you have believed it? That I could say behind your back that you looked like a trussed chicken in your confirmation dress?' He shook his head helplessly. 'I thought you looked beautiful that day. I *told* you you looked beautiful. Don't you remember that?'

'Yes. But then, afterwards, Hamish told me...' Emotion rushed through her. Her voice began to crack. 'Did you really not say all those terrible things? Was it really all a lie? Did you never really hate me?'

A look of pain crossed his face. He breathed in deeply. Then he rose to his feet, drawing her up with him.

'Oh, Fiona...'

She trembled as his arms went round her, pulling her close to him, his lips in her hair.

'I never hated you. I loved you as a little sister. Until——'

As he paused, her heart slammed against her ribs. She hardly dared listen to what he was about to say next.

But she was going to have to listen. He was pulling gently away from her, holding her at arm's length, gazing into her face. 'Until you grew up. Then my feelings changed. I didn't love you any more as a little sister. I loved you as a man loves a woman.'

Fiona could feel happiness stealing up on her, but she dared not quite believe it. She looked up at him, her frightened, loving heart in her eyes.

He brushed the hair from her forehead, making her shiver. 'But you hated me, and who can blame you? That was something I was very sure of—at least, until a couple of days ago at Aviemore——'

As he broke off, she felt a melting deep inside her to see the emotion shining naked and raw from his eyes. She touched his cheek with the back of her finger. 'I love you, Craig. I always have. I only hated you out of self-defence. Deep down, I think I always loved you.'

Something shifted in his eyes. 'How? As a big brother?'

Fiona took a deep breath. 'Yes. When I was a child. Then I loved you as a big brother.' She smiled. 'But I haven't been a child for quite a while.' Her ribs felt so tight she could scarcely breathe. She touched his face again. 'I love you, Craig. I love you as a woman loves a man.'

He drew her to him then and held her tightly, as though he would never again, for all time, let her go.

He breathed against her hair, 'Marry me, Fiona. Marry me and bear my children. Marry me and help me run my empire.' He looked into her eyes and smiled an almost desperate smile. 'Marry me and make me the happiest man alive.'

Fiona looked back at him, her soul weeping with happiness, her heart floating only a little lower than the angels.

'Of course,' she answered. 'Of course I'll marry you.'

Then he was gathering her into his arms, bending to kiss her, and suddenly there was no more darkness, no more sorrow. She was standing on a mountain-top, with Craig beside her, about to plunge into a bright new future, safe in his arms, surrounded by his love.

Make Christmas a truly
Romantic experience—with

HARLEQUIN ROMANCE®

Wouldn't *you* love to kiss a tall, dark
Texan under the mistletoe? Gwen does,
in HOME FOR CHRISTMAS by
Ellen James. Share the experience!

Wouldn't *you* love to kiss a sexy
New Englander on a snowy Christmas
morning? Angela does, in Shannon
Waverly's CHRISTMAS ANGEL.
Share the experience!

Look for both of these Christmas
Romance titles, available in December
wherever Harlequin Books are sold.

(And don't forget that Romance novels
make great gifts! Easy to buy, easy to
wrap and just the right size for a
stocking stuffer. And they make a
wonderful treat when you need a break
from Christmas shopping, Christmas
wrapping and stuffing stockings!)

©DG 1990   HRXT

1993 Keepsake

CHRISTMAS

Stories

Capture the spirit and romance of Christmas with KEEPSAKE CHRISTMAS STORIES, a collection of three stories by favorite historical authors. The perfect Christmas gift!

Don't miss these heartwarming stories, available in November wherever Harlequin books are sold:

ONCE UPON A CHRISTMAS by Curtiss Ann Matlock
A FAIRYTALE SEASON by Marianne Willman
TIDINGS OF JOY by Victoria Pade

ADD A TOUCH OF ROMANCE TO YOUR HOLIDAY SEASON WITH KEEPSAKE CHRISTMAS STORIES!

HX93

MEN MADE IN AMERICA

Fifty red-blooded, white-hot, true-blue hunks
from every State in the Union!

Look for MEN MADE IN AMERICA! Written by some
of our most poplar authors, these stories feature fifty of
the strongest, sexiest men, each from a different state in
the union!

Two titles available every other month at your favorite
retail outlet.

In November, look for:

**STRAIGHT FROM THE HEART by Barbara Delinsky
(Connecticut)
AUTHOR'S CHOICE by Elizabeth August (Delaware)**

In January, look for:

**DREAM COME TRUE by Ann Major (Florida)
WAY OF THE WILLOW by Linda Shaw (Georgia)**

You won't be able to resist MEN MADE IN AMERICA!